Hot-Tempered Farmers

The Case of the Barbecued Barns

Chuck Harwood

**LEARNING
TRIANGLE
PRESS**

*Connecting
kids, parents, and teachers
through learning*

An imprint of McGraw-Hill
New York San Francisco Washington, D.C. Auckland Bogotá Caracas
Lisbon London Madrid Mexico City Milan Montreal New Delhi
San Juan Singapore Sydney Tokyo Toronto

McGraw-Hill

A Division of The **McGraw·Hill** Companies

Library of Congress Cataloging-in-Publication Data applied for.

1 2 3 4 5 6 7 8 9 0 DOC/DOC 9 0 2 1 0 9 8 7

ISBN 0-07-006389-3

The sponsoring editor for this book was Judith Terrill-Breuer, the senior producer was Joe Shepherd, the editing supervisor was Patricia V. Amoroso, and the production supervisor was Claire B. Stanley. It was set in Century Old Style by Jaclyn J. Boone of McGraw-Hill's Professional Book Group in Hightstown, New Jersey.

Printed and bound by R.R. Donnelley & Sons Company.

Contents

About the Crew

It is the near future. Peace has broken out all over the world, and the President of the United States has decided to donate the world's most sophisticated military vehicle, the X-100 Advanced Tactical Vehicle, to "the youth of America, that they might use this powerful tool to learn, to explore, and to help others."

Since the X-100 was designed in a top-secret factory in Kinetic City, the vehicle was renamed **The Kinetic City Express** and the first young crew was dubbed the **Kinetic City Super Crew**.

But who would be the members of the Crew? Kinetic City's mayor, Richard M. Schwindle, puts out a call to the young people of the city. Many answer the call, and seven are chosen: Keisha, Derek, Megan, Curtis, Fernando, PJ, and Max.

Now the Crew travel the world, along with their talkative supercomputer, ALEC, in a tireless quest for truth, justice, and the perfect deep-dish pizza. Their quest may never end.

About the Train

CIA Top Secret Document #113057
DECLASSIFIED: 9/12/99

Originally designed to carry military intelligence teams to trouble spots throughout the world, the X-100 is capable of ultra-high-speed travel, under the control of the Advanced Logic Electronic Computer (ALEC) Series 9000. The vehicle can travel over land on existing train tracks and on tank-style treads. For crossing bodies of water, the X-100 can seal its waterproof bulkheads and travel underwater, using an advanced form of Magneto-Hydrodynamic Drive propulsion. The X-100 has several small vehicles within it which can travel with or without human passengers, including a small submarine and a jet copter. Finally, the X-100 has sophisticated information-gathering capabilities, using 'round-the-clock, high-speed access to the Internet, an extensive CD-ROM library, and the ability to generate realistic science simulations in its "Cyber Car."

The Phone Call

"Kinetic City Super Crew. When you want the facts, we hit the tracks. Curtis speaking."

"This is Lilliette McDog! You've got to help us out in Vegtaville!"

"Uh oh. What's the problem?"

"Two barns have burned down! It could reignite the old feud!"

"What old feud?"

"The one between the Catfields and the McDogs! Hurry up before it's too late!"

CHAPTER ONE

A Case Too Hot to Handle?

Kinetic City Express Journal: hot-tempered Farmers, or the Case of the Barbecued Barns. Curtis reporting. It had been a slow summer day on the KC Express Train until Lilliette McDog gave us an urgent call on the KC Hotline. Around noon the day before, her family's brand new barn mysteriously burned down to the ground. A few hours later, their neighbor's new barn suspiciously went up in flames as well! All that was left of either barn now was just a big pile of smoking ashes. While this was bad enough, it was made even worse by the fact that the McDogs and their neighbors, the Catfields, didn't get along. They both owned large dairy farms in the small town of Vegtaville, and were in constant competition with each other. In fact, the two families had been feuding for almost fifty years!

Even before the smoke cleared from the latest barn burnings, the McDogs and the Catfields were hurling accusations of arson across the property line. Each side was convinced the other had burned their barn on purpose. However, not everyone within the families was angry. In fact, just the opposite. Lilliette McDog and Robby Joe Catfield were in love and secretly engaged to be married. Until the barns burned down, the young couple had been hoping the announcement of their wedding plans would end the bad feelings between their families once and for all. But, with tempers flaring and sparks flying, the young lovebirds didn't know what to do. If their parents found out about the engagement now, there was no telling what might happen. That's why Lilliette turned to us for help. She was convinced it wasn't arson and, if we could prove it, then maybe she and Robby Joe could get married and help end the old feud once and for all.

As soon as I got off the hotline, I rushed off to gather the rest of the Super Crew. I found Keisha in the Music Car practicing her saxophone; Derek in the Gym Car doing sit-ups; and Megan in the Laboratory Car checking out my latest inventions for possible investment opportunities. I quickly told everybody what was up. Then we met back in the KC Express' Control Car. That's our train's nerve center and the place we always meet to talk about our new cases. It's also home for our fast-talking computer, ALEC. Keisha, Derek, and I got there first . . .

"I don't know, Curtis," Keisha said. "I'm usually gung-ho about our cases, but do we really want to get in the middle of a family feud?"

Derek nodded. "Yeah. Especially one

between the Catfields and McDogs. My dad grew up in Vegtaville. From what he told me, a fight between those two families can get pretty ugly."

The Control Car door *shwooshed* open, and Megan came walking in.

"This case sounds great," she said excitedly. "I'm already thinking of my headlines."

"What headlines?" Derek asked.

"For the story I'll write for the *National Tattler*, of course!" Megan responded.

That was classic Megan. She's always thinking about ways to become rich and famous. The *National Tattler* is her favorite tabloid. Their slogan? "We have a nose for news, and we'll stick it where it stinks!" Needless to say, the *National Tattler* wasn't exactly the most reliable source for information.

"How about 'Feuding Farmers Fight Fire with Fire'?" Megan asked. "Or, 'All Vegtaville's Cooked to a Crisp!' or 'Ghost of Elvis Appears in Flaming Barn!!'"

Megan's excitement soon caught hold of Keisha. Whatever doubts she had about getting involved, they were no match for her love of a good, juicy mystery.

"You know, maybe we SHOULD go check this one out," she said. "It's been too quiet around here lately. We could use a little danger, action, and adventure."

Without meaning to, Keisha's words sent a cold shiver up my spine. Don't misunderstand. It's not that I'm a total chicken. It's just that, if given a choice between risking my neck on a case or tinkering with my inventions in the Lab Car, I'd say hand me some pliers and a pile of old kitchen appliances and watch me create.

"Um, hold on a second, everybody," I said. "I like danger, action, and adventure as much as the next person . . ."

Megan giggled. "Yeah, Curtis. If the next person is Mr. Rogers."

I ignored her and continued my thought. "But this case may be TOO hot to handle! I mean, what if someone tries to set fire to the

KC Express train?"

"Don't worry, Curtis," Megan spoke up confidently. "We can always hold them off with this!"

She pulled her hands from behind her back and held up my latest invention, the Thermo-launcher. She had snuck it in from the Lab Car to surprise Derek and Keisha. It worked; their eyes grew wide at once.

"Megan!" Keisha shouted. "Put that bazooka away right now!"

Megan started laughing, and I figured I had better explain things quickly before we had a feud of our own. Keisha and Derek would blow their tops if they thought it was a real weapon.

"That's not a bazooka," I said. "It's a thermometer."

"It's a what?" Derek asked, making sure he had heard correctly.

"A thermometer," I repeated. "I call it the 'Thermo-launcher.' It only looks like a bazooka because the barrel's made out of an old pipe.

I found it in the train's plumbing works."

"Hey," Keisha said. "No wonder the toilet isn't flushing!"

"Ha ha," I said. "Of course I wouldn't take it from the toilet pipe. I cut a section from the tube that carries the train's brake fluid."

The rest of the Crew looked at me wide-eyed.

"Just kidding," I assured them.

They breathed out a sigh of relief.

"You see, inside the tube there's a thermometer attached to some fishing line. When you pull the trigger, a spring sends it flying out, and the reel behind the trigger hauls it back in, just like a fishing rod. Want to give it a shot, Keisha?"

She placed the Thermo-launcher on her shoulder like she had just landed a role in an action film.

"Who wants their temperature taken?" she asked in a macho voice.

"Very funny," I said. "Why don't you take the temperature of the potted plant over there instead?"

"Okay," Keisha said smiling. I'll see how warm the soil is."

Keisha turned toward our little lemon tree in the far corner of the Control Car. CLICK! —she pulled the trigger. KA-CHUNK!!!— the thermometer flew out of the barrel. THWUMP!!—it sank deep into the dirt around the potted plant.

"Bull's eye!" Megan called out. "Good shot, Keisha!"

"Thanks," Keisha said. "But I still don't understand. What's the point of a Thermo-launcher in the first place?"

"What do you mean?" I said. "There're all kinds of things you can do with it."

"For example?" Derek asked.

"Well . . ." I had to think about it a second, "you can take the temperature of the water in the deep end of the pool before jumping off the board," I responded. "Or, if you're at the beach, you can find out how hot the sand is before running across it barefoot."

Keisha and Derek looked at me like I was a little nuts. They didn't always understand that an inventor sometimes invents just for the fun of it.

"Maybe we can even use it to measure people's tempers out in Vegtaville," Megan suggested with a laugh.

That reminded me of Lilliette. She had told me stuff on the phone that the Crew still didn't know about.

"Hold on," I said. "Lilliette McDog is sure no one burned anything. In fact, her parents are more upset about being accused of arson than they are about their barn burning down."

"Maybe," Derek said. "But what about the Catfields? How does Lilliette know that one of them didn't start the fires?"

"Because," I explained, "she and Robby Joe Catfield are secretly engaged to be married."

"Aww, that's so sweet," Keisha said. "It's just like that Shakespeare play I read in English class last year, 'Romeo and Juliet.' You see, it was all about this young couple in love, but their families kept feuding with one another until . . ."

"Ahem," Derek coughed in that little way he does when we start straying off the subject. "That's a great play, but let's talk about it some other time. Right now we have a case to crack."

"Oh yeah, the case," Keisha said, looking back at me. "So Lilliette's sure no one from the Catfield side started those fires, huh?"

"That's right," I nodded. "Robby Joe gave her a promise and that's what she believes."

"But how do we know Robby Joe is telling the truth?" Derek said.

"We don't," I admitted.

"We'll have to keep an open mind," Keisha added. "We can't rule anything out yet."

"What did their families do when Lilliette and Robby Joe said it wasn't arson?" Megan asked.

"Lilliette says they looked at them like they were nuts," I answered. "Their parents are just too angry to believe them."

"Hmm," Derek said, thinking out loud, "if

we can't solve this one with our heads, the Catfields and McDogs might try to solve it with their fists."

"Derek's right," Keisha said, pulling a notebook out of a drawer. "But if we are going to find some other explanation for this, we'd better start brainstorming. Let's make a list of other ways those fires may have started."

"How about a cigarette?" I said, looking at Megan.

"Curtis?!" she said surprised. "I don't smoke!"

I started to laugh. Megan had fallen for my joke.

"I don't think he means for you, Megan," Keisha laughed. "I think he means maybe someone tossed away a burning cigarette. If it landed in some hay—PHOOF!! Instant fire."

"Yeah. Good thinking," Derek agreed. "I've heard cigarettes cause lots of fires."

"So cigarettes definitely go on the list," Keisha said as she wrote it down. "What else?"

"What about those big storms we've been

having the last couple of days?" I suggested.

That one was too good for Megan to pass up. She pounced on it at once.

"Good thinking, Curtis," she said. "The rain did it!"

"Ha ha," I said. "Very funny, Megan. Not the rain—the lightning. I read that's how ancient people probably got fire in the first place."

"I don't know," Derek said, shaking his head slowly. "Lightning hitting both of those barns in one week would be quite a coincidence."

"Right," Keisha agreed. "But let's include it anyway. It's still possible."

"Did Lilliette have any clues, Curtis?" Megan asked.

I shook my head. "Nope. She just said that one day their brand new barn was standing. The next day their Ultra Comfort Suite was just a big heap of ashes."

"Their *what* was just a big heap of ashes?" Derek asked.

"Their Ultra Comfort Suite," I answered. "Both the Catfields and McDogs had just bought one. They're supposed to be the coolest digs a cow could ever wish for."

"Oh yeah," Megan said. "Now I remember. I read about Ultra Comfort Suites in the *National Tattler's* business section. A company called Paradise Barns makes them. They're a division of Gawdy Gadjets, Inc."

Derek rubbed his chin, a sure sign he was thinking as hard as he could.

"Well, if those barns were exactly alike," he said, "then maybe there's something wrong with the way they were made, like bad electric wiring or something."

Keisha nodded her head as she wrote. "Good point. A new and untested kind of barn. That gives us three possibilities already. Anything else?"

"Why don't we fire up ALEC the computer and ask him?" Megan suggested. "Maybe he can give us some ideas we haven't thought of."

"Good idea," Keisha said, putting down her

notebook and sitting in front of ALEC's keyboard. "He's got the hottest circuits around."

As she began to type, the rest of us turned our attention to the big screen monitor that fills up an entire wall of the Control Car. ALEC is one of the world's most powerful computers and definitely one of the coolest. Not only can he give us information on practically any subject imaginable, but he also controls the KC Express Train and can whisk us anywhere in the world we want to go. Not that ALEC isn't without his faults, of course. He's programed to be as human as possible, which means that he can be quirky. For example, his excitement sometimes gets the best of him. At other times, he can almost seem like his feelings are hurt, especially if he doesn't feel like he's being useful to us. Still, ALEC has so much personality that we consider him our friend and wouldn't trade him for anything. We just don't tell him, that's all. Otherwise it would go to his circuits.

"Hellllooooo, Crew!" ALEC chirped as he

came on. "Did you know that the center of the Earth has a temperature over 8,000 degrees?! That's hot enough to melt a lead snowball."

"Funny you should mention heat, ALEC," Keisha said. "We have a four-alarm emergency right now! There've been some mysterious barn burnings."

ALEC beeped twice, a sure sign he had something important for us.

"You mean those barns owned by the Catfields and McDogs?" he asked.

Our jaws dropped in amazement. We knew ALEC was brilliant, but we didn't think he could read minds.

"How . . . how did you know that?" I asked, not sure I even wanted to hear the answer.

"Oh. Simple," ALEC replied, punctuating it with a few happy sounding beeps. "Even while my voice activation program is off, my memory banks still pick up and store news broadcasts. That's why, when you need me for a case, I'm already stuffed with the stuff you need to know!"

"Cool ALEC," Derek said admiringly. "But what station has been talking about the Catfields and McDogs?"

"Radio W.A.R.N.," he answered.

"Oh no!" we all said at once.

Radio W.A.R.N. didn't just broadcast emergencies, it did its best to cause them!

"Shall I play back their last public announcement for you, Crew?" ALEC asked. "I have it stored in my audio files."

"I'm almost afraid to hear it," Derek said. "But sure. We need to know exactly what we're up against."

After three short beeps from ALEC's speakers, we were tuned to the prerecorded broadcast.

"You're listening to W.A.R.N.—all disasters, all the time! Well, it looks like all-out warfare's coming this summer to the town of Vegtaville! After warming up with a little arson, the Catfields and McDogs appear all set for a few rounds of mindless violence! The whole thing began with a competition to supply the

Mellow Milk company with milk from comfy cattle. Now it looks like the only competition will be which family can fling the biggest bull biscuits! Word has it that both families are building GIANT CATAPULTS at this very moment! I don't know about you, but Radio W.A.R.N.'s betting the Catfields and McDogs won't be using them to trade recipes! So stay tuned for all the exciting action as we bring you the latest scoop on the flying poop! Only on W.A.R.N., all disasters, all the time!"

"Yeech," Keisha said as ALEC clicked it off. "That has to be the slimiest station ever."

"I know what you mean," Derek agreed. "Every time I hear it, I feel like I need to take a shower."

"I don't know," Megan said. "I kind of like it."

We all groaned.

"Hey, come on! It's sort of the *National Tattler* of the airwaves," Megan said, defending her tastes.

We all groaned again.

"Hey, you've got to admit," Megan added, "it is entertaining."

"Yeah, like a mud wrestling match," I said.

"Let's concentrate on the case, Crew," Derek broke in. "If that report on Radio W.A.R.N. is true, it's more important than ever to figure out how those fires really started."

"Speaking of fires starting," ALEC chimed back in, "did you know one of the biggest causes of accidental fire is burning cigarettes? Or there's lightning, that's also a possibility. Or how about bad electric wiring? Did you know . . ."

"ALEC," we all shouted at once.

"What? What?" he asked.

"Um . . . thanks for your suggestions," Keisha said carefully. "But we already thought of all those."

"Oh," ALEC said softly, sounding hurt. "I see. Well . . . it looks like you don't really need me anymore. All right. I can take it. I'm a big computer. Curtis, if you would be so kind as to drag my operating system into the trash icon and hit 'delete,' I'll be out of your lives for good."

"ALEC, we're NOT going to delete you!" I said.

"Fine," he replied, "I'll do it myself then. That way I won't needlessly repeat what you've already thought ... WAIT!!!! Have you considered flammable liquids?!"

We all shook our heads while Derek spoke up.

"Flammable liquids? Actually, ALEC we hadn't thought of ..."

"YES!!!!" ALEC boomed out at the top of his speakers, sending out beeps, bells, and whistles in the process. "You see Crew? You need me after all! And to think you were about to delete me."

"We would've been lost without you, ALEC," Megan said. "So, what's this stuff about flammable liquids?"

ALEC let out a long, proud trumpet blast before responding.

"Substances such as gasoline or paint thinner pose a serious fire risk. If they aren't stored properly, their fumes can collect near the floor, and even a small spark can set off a big bang."

"Wow! That might just be it!" Keisha said.

Excited as ever, ALEC continued without pause, "And, speaking of the Big Bang, did you know that many scientists think the Universe exploded into existence about 15 billion years ago? That's over a hundred billion in dog years! And speaking of dogs . . ."

"Uh, thanks ALEC," Derek said quickly, cutting him off. "But we have to get out to the case in a hurry!"

"Right!" Megan agreed, "ALEC, set course for Vegtaville!"

"No problem, Crew!" he replied between his happiest beeps. "I'll have you out to those barn burnings in a flash!"

CHAPTER TWO

Cyber Fire!

We had a few minutes to spare as our super train sped out to Vegtaville, so we decided to pay a quick visit to the Cyber Car for an inside view on how fires get started. The Control Car may be the most important car on our train, but the Cyber Car is definitely the coolest. It's equipped with all the latest technology in virtual reality, including Surround Sound headphones, True View Goggles, and Real Feel Gloves. There are even special, padded platforms for us to stand on. They have sensors in the floor and can move in any direction. All the fancy gadgets make the programs as lifelike as possible. In fact, they can sometimes even seem too real and get a little scary. But then again, that's part of the fun . . .

"Welcome to the Cyber Car!" our automatic door said as it opened with a *swoosh*. "Please watch your step!"

I could see Keisha and Derek smirking. They thought the 'daily safety message' program I had put in the talking doors was a little weird. But they pretty much just ignored the helpful hints. Megan, on the other hand, just couldn't get used to being talked to by a door. It kind of freaked her out.

"Remember to floss after meals," the door said helpfully to Megan as she followed us in. "Especially after eating fresh spinach. It sticks between the teeth."

"Uh . . . Okay" Megan said, sounding a little uncomfortable. I had to admit, I might have given the program a little too much power. The doors were beginning to sound like my mother. Luckily, the awkward moment passed quickly as ALEC's automatic sensors picked us up and sprang him to life.

"Heelllooo Crew! So what will it be today? A glass elevator ride to the center of the Earth?

A submarine voyage through a frog's digestive system?"

"Um . . . sounds interesting, ALEC," Derek responded, "but not today. We need to know more about accidental fires."

"Then you're in luck!" ALEC chirped happily, glad to be of service. "I recently downloaded a frightful program of a bedroom fire. Through the amazing technology of virtual reality, you can watch the fire from inside a burning bedroom! That's something you could never do in real life."

"No kidding," I agreed. "You'd be fried."

"Correct!" ALEC said as he chimed an electronic bell. "Also, in real life, you couldn't see anything from inside a bedroom fire. There would be far too much thick, suffocating smoke. But, with virtual reality, I can give you a clear view from inside the flames!"

"Wow! Sounds hot!" Keisha said.

"Sounds scary," I added.

"You bet!" ALEC said. "Just put on your cyber goggles, and you'll find yourself . . ."

"In one seriously messy bedroom," Megan broke in. She was standing on her platform and had already switched her goggles on. "Who does the cleaning around here, a pack of preschoolers on a sugar rush?"

"Looks okay to me," I said. I had no problem with a messy room. Just the opposite. When done well, it could even be a kind of art form.

"Is this the bedroom that's about to be burned to a crisp, ALEC?" Derek asked.

"Sure is!" he confirmed.

"How would anybody notice?" Megan muttered under her breath.

"In fact," ALEC continued, "the fire has already been going for one and a half minutes."

That surprised us completely. Everything on our cyber-goggle screens looked normal.

"Where is it, ALEC?" I asked.

Derek spoke up first.

"Oh, there it is. On the bed. You can just see some little puffs of smoke coming up."

I had been expecting a raging inferno.

"That's it?! That's the big, scary fire?!"

"Remember, Curtis," ALEC said, "almost all accidental fires start like this. In this case, a burning cigarette has been left on the bed."

"Hey," Megan called out, "I think I just saw a little flame jump up."

"Oooh," Keisha said excitedly. "I'm getting goose bumps. We're getting closer to the scary part!"

I walked over to the messy bed. From there I could see the burning cigarette. It rested on top of some plaid sheets covered with a pattern of green maple leaves. As I looked, another small orange flame shot up from the sheets.

"Yep. The bed is definitely on fire all right." I said, stepping back as close as I could to the door. I like fire about as much as I like snakes and spiders.

"Okay, Crew," ALEC explained, "we have open flame at the two-minute mark. Now allow me to fast-forward a little so you can see the fire grow more quickly than it would in real life."

WHOOOOOOOSH!!!!

"Whoa!!," we all shouted as the entire bed erupted into flames. Even though we knew it was just virtual reality, standing in a burning bedroom is about as scary as it gets. The fire was spreading quickly. One flame ignited the box of tissues on the nightstand. Another leapt up from the pillow and caught hold of some movie posters tacked to the wall. We watched spellbound as Darth Vader's Death Star got burned once again.

"Notice the smoke rising up to the ceiling, Crew," ALEC said, sounding just as calm as he did before. "Smoke is a mixture of particles and hot gases, a combination that is lighter than the rest of the air in the room."

"Oh, so that's why you're supposed to crawl through a room that's on fire," Keisha broke in. "The cool, clean air's closer to the floor."

"You got it, Keisha!" ALEC confirmed.

"Wow! Look!" I said, pointing to the flames. "They're starting to shoot way up the wall!"

"Exactly," ALEC added. "As we speak, that flame on the bed is heating up everything in the room—the chair, the carpet, even the wallpaper. All of these things can get so hot that they'll burst into flames!"

"What?" Derek sounded surprised. "You mean things don't have to touch the flame to catch on fire?"

"That's right, Derek," ALEC said. "If something gets hotter than a certain temperature, it can ignite on its own. That's why we call that temperature the ignition point. It's different for every object. For example, most paper will burst into flames if it's heated to 451 degrees Fahrenheit."

"Check it out. It's smoking like a chimney!"

I nodded my head, "Yeah, and look at the . . ."

WHOOOOOOOOOOOOOOOOOOOOOOOOS SSSSSSSSSHHHHHHH!!!!!!!!!!!

We all screamed as the room ignited like a lit match dropped on a puddle of gasoline! Where a second before there had been furniture, there was now only a huge sheet of orange flame ripping through the ceiling and shooting high into the attic.

"What happened, ALEC?!" I called out, my voice shaking a little. "Did you give us the bedroom nuclear bomb test by mistake?"

"No mistake, Curtis," ALEC responded as cheerfully as ever. "What you just saw is called *flashover*. The burning bed filled the room with super-heated gases. If things get hot enough, those gases can explode. That's why you must exit immediately if there's a fire and not go back in for any reason."

"So what do we do now, ALEC?" Derek asked.

"Well, if this were a real fire and you were somewhere in the building, what do you think you should do?"

"*Escape*!!" we all shouted at once.

"Right! I'll transfer you to another room so you can have a fighting chance. If you had really been in the flashover room . . . well, there wouldn't be much of a point anymore, if you know what I mean."

There was a quick blur across our cyber goggles as ALEC electronically whisked us to another part of the burning building.

"So what do we do now, Crew?" Megan asked.

I looked around. We were in another bedroom. There weren't any flames, but there sure was a lot of smoke. It collected near the ceiling in a hot gray fog.

"Get on your hands and knees, everybody!" Keisha yelled. "We've got to stay under the smoke!"

I got down on all fours and felt the automatic treadmill kick in. Even though I knew I was perfectly safe, crawling around on the floor like that sure seemed real enough. Thanks to the Real Feel gloves, I could even feel the carpet.

"Look for the doors and windows!" Keisha suggested.

"Hey, I see a window!" Derek called out. Maybe we can get out that way."

Keisha got to it first.

"Oh no!" she said, "we're three stories up!"

"We'll have to find the door that leads to the stairs," I said.

"Yeah," Derek agreed, "but which one's that? I see two of them and they're both closed."

"I'll try this one," I said, crawling toward it.

"Wait!" Keisha yelled out, just in time. "Don't grab the handle!"

"Why not?" I asked.

"Because if the fire's on the other side of it, it'll burn your hand!"

"Keisha's right!" Derek said. "The metal conducts the heat. Touch the wood near the bottom!"

I reached out and felt it with my virtual reality glove. ALEC really had the juice turned up. The virtual door actually felt hot. I pulled my hand away as quickly as I could.

"It's burning up!" I told the others.

"Then the bedroom fire must be on the other side!" Megan said.

"Quick, Derek," Keisha called out, "try

the other door!"

"Check!" he said as he crawled over to touch it.

"If that one's hot, too," I said, "I'm taking off my Cyber Goggles and running to the Pool Car."

"We're in luck," Derek said, holding his hand to the wood. "This one's still cool."

"Go ahead!" Keisha said. "Open it!"

Derek did.

"The stairs!" we all shouted.

"C'mon, Crew!" Keisha shouted as she crawled for the door, "let's get out of here!"

We didn't need much encouragement.

"Remember everybody," Derek called out, "stay on your hands and knees until it's safe."

I made it halfway downstairs before standing up carefully. "Hey, it's all clear now."

"Last one out is a hard-boiled egg!" Keisha called out.

We raced each other out the front door and into safety. A good thing, too. Not more than five seconds after we got out and turned around, the top stories of the house were engulfed in a huge ball of flame! As our cyber goggles slowly went blank and the sound effects died down, ALEC switched his voice back to the speaker mounted on the Cyber Car wall.

"Congratulations, Crew!" he said. "That was less than twenty seconds. Perfectly done! It makes me proud to be your computer!"

"Thanks, ALEC," Megan said.

"And that's the end of your cyber adventure. According to my instruments, we'll be arriving in Vegtaville in less than two minutes. Please return your cyber goggles to their locked and upright position."

"Let's go, Crew!" Keisha said as she ran out the door. "We've got a case to crack!"

Derek and I followed close behind her. As the last one out, Megan stopped to turn out the lights.

"Oh, I'll get that, Megan," the Cyber Car door said to her pleasantly. "You just go and have a nice time."

"Uh . . . thank you," we heard her reply.

"And remember, an untied shoe is a dangerous shoe!"

"I'll try and keep it in mind," she said, sounding a little sarcastic.

I knew what was coming. Megan tapped me on the shoulder when she caught up.

"Hey Curtis, could you deactivate the door's voice program? " she asked. "It weirds me out."

I would've answered her, but I was laughing too hard.

CHAPTER THREE

A Close Call

The KC Express let us off about a quarter mile from the McDog's dairy farm. Lilliette had given me instructions on the exact place to meet her—the McDog's old storage shed. Since it was far away from the main house, it seemed like a good place to hold a secret meeting. We crawled very carefully under a barbed-wire fence and walked through a field of cows. Following Lilliette's directions, we soon came to a warehouse-like building made out of sheet metal . . .

"Is this the place she told you about, Curtis?" Keisha asked.

I nodded my head. "Yeah. It's light green with a pond beside it. Just like Lilliette said."

"So where's Lilliette?" Megan asked.

Derek walked across the gravel and knocked on the shed's door.

"Super Crew?" a soft, quiet voice called out as the door swung open a crack.

"Lilliette?" Derek said.

"Uh huh," she replied from the darkness. "Quick. Come inside before anyone sees you."

The door opened wider, and we all stepped in. After a couple of seconds, our eyes got used to the dim light and we could see Lilliette. She stood in front of us, wearing denim work clothes and a baseball cap over her frizzy red hair. We had just finished introducing ourselves when I let out a gasp. Suddenly, my fear of getting scratched, stung, kicked, or bitten overcame my desire to look cool.

"Hey!" I said nervously, "th . . .this place is full of animals!"

Everyone looked in the direction I pointed. Along the far side of the wall, figures of horses, pigs, ducks, dogs, and chickens stood out from the shadows. For some weird reason, they were all standing totally still without making a sound. Lilliette quickly explained before we all freaked out.

"Oh, don't worry about them, Crew. They're just plastic models."

"Models?" Derek repeated. "Why do you need those? They're enough animals running around here to make Old McDonald jealous."

"I know what you mean," Lilliette said. "But the Paradise Barns company gave them to us when we bought the very first Ultra Comfort Suite. They're supposed to be decorations. You know, kind of like those plastic flamingos people put on their lawns."

"Why did you buy an Ultra Comfort Suite in the first place?" Keisha asked. "Did it have anything to do with that Mellow Milk contest we heard about on Radio W.A.R.N.?"

"You bet your donkey it does," Lilliette responded. "Mellow Milk is a big dairy company that buys only organic milk from happy cows."

"What's the point of that?" Derek asked.

"Haven't you heard?" Megan asked. "It's just like free-range chickens. There's a hot market for all-natural dairy products. I read about it in the *National Tattler*'s business section. Organic milk from comfy cows goes for big bucks."

"Exactly," Lilliette said. "And Mellow Milk is having a competition to see who can raise the happiest, most comfortable cows in the county. Whoever wins will get that Mellow Milk money. That's why both our families bought those Ultra Comfort Suites. They're awfully expensive, but they're the only barns luxurious enough to stand a chance in the contest."

"I'm beginning to see why the old feud's heating back up," Keisha broke in. "With that big Mellow Milk contract on the line, it's easy to believe those fires were set on purpose."

"Uh huh," Lilliette agreed. She wiped a lone tear away with the sleeve of her shirt. "In fact, our families are so mad at each other, they're building a wall between our farms."

"Well, that doesn't sound that bad . . ." I said.

"Oh yeah?" she responded. "It's ten feet high with razor wire on top! Even worse, they're making catapults as well."

"Catapults?" Derek repeated. "So what Radio W.A.R.N. said is true."

"Aren't catapults a little old fashioned?" Megan asked.

"I guess," Lilliette said. "But believe me, they can still do plenty of damage. Besides, if we used guns, it would end the feud *permanently*, though not in a way any of us could live with—if you know what I mean. That's why catapults have become sort of a Catfield and McDog tradition. My brothers and sisters have been combing the farm all morning, looking for ammo to lob."

"Oh no!" I said, partly because I felt bad for Lilliette and partly because it was starting to sound dangerous.

"We've got to solve this case," Derek said. "If we can prove it's not arson, maybe we can stop the latest round of this catapult contest from starting."

A hopeful look crossed Lilliette's face. "Oh,

please do, Super Crew! Robby Joe and I tried to stop them this morning, but it was no use. His parents are just as stubborn as mine. Plus they have Colonel Stonewall Catfield egging them on."

"Who's he?" Keisha asked.

"He's Robby Joe's grandpa. He's dying to get back at my grandma, Lady Margaret McDog."

"Why would he want to do that?" Keisha asked.

Lilliette sighed. "Well, it's kind of a long story. But, a long time ago, our families were really close. In fact, Colonel Catfield and Lady McDog were going to get married."

"So, what happened?" Derek asked.

"Well, no one likes to talk about it," Lilliette admitted, "but from what Robby Joe and I have been able to figure out, Lady Margaret left him standing at the altar."

"Wow, your grandma jilted him, huh?!" Keisha said. "That's cold."

"But I know for a fact she wanted to marry him," Lilliette protested. "It's just that the horse got sick on the way to the wedding and couldn't pull the buggy. Lady Margaret and her brother got out and walked the last three miles, but, by the time they got to the chapel, everyone was gone."

"So why didn't your grandma just explain things later?" Megan asked.

"She was going to," Lilliette said, "but Colonel Catfield got so angry when she didn't show up he wrote her a nasty note. I even found it in the attic not too long ago."

"What did the note say?" Derek asked.

Lilliette repeated from memory. "Dear 'Lady' Margaret, pity you didn't show up at the wedding this morning. I was going to marry your horse. It has better teeth."

"Ouch," I said.

"So, in a nutshell," Derek said, "Lady Margaret and Colonel Catfield both think the other one dissed them at the altar."

"Uh huh," Lilliette nodded sadly. "And that's how this whole stupid feud got started. It was cooling down for a while. But now, with these barn burnings, things are worse than ever. If our families find out about Robby Joe and me, there's no telling what might happen."

"Gosh, what a sad story," Keisha said.

She wasn't the only one who thought so. It was obvious the talk of the tragic love affair and the inflamed feud had made Lilliette upset, too. But she didn't have time to start crying. Footsteps and angry voices suddenly filled the air, growing louder and louder. Lilliette's eyes widened. People were coming into the storage shed!

"Quick! Hide!" she said. "My family's coming. I don't want them to know I've called you on the case! They have such bad tempers!"

Derek glanced around the shed. "But where!?"

Lilliette bit her lip nervously as she looked around. "Um . . . there! In back of the plastic horses! Hurry!"

We all ran to the far side of the storage shed and jumped behind a pair of lifesized plastic horses just in time. The door flew open wide as Mr. McDog marched in, followed by all of Lilliette's sisters and brothers. We quickly realized they had one thing on their minds—ammunition!

"Okay!" Mr. McDog bellowed out, "everybody grab somethin' for the catapult. Marsha, Jan, Cindy, why don't you all get a bunch of those big plastic chickens Paradise Barns gave us."

"Okay, dad." "Right, pop," we heard Lilliette's little sisters say as they began to gather ammo.

"Greg, Peter, Bobby," Mr. McDog continued, "come on over here and help me with these horses."

"Uh oh," I heard Derek whisper.

"Wait, dad!" Lilliette said, stepping out from the shadows just in the nick of time.

"Lilliette," Mr. McDog said. "What are you doing in here? You should be out helpin' your cousins build our wall!"

"Um . . . I'm um . . ." Lilliette searched for words, "uh . . . looking for ammo! Yeah, that's it!

I'm looking for catapult ammo!"

"That's my girl," her father said proudly. "So what do you figure we should use?"

Lilliette had to think quickly. Greg, Peter and Bobby were already picking up the first horse. If they grabbed the one in front of us, we'd have a lot of uncomfortable explaining to do. She came through for us with a stroke of genius.

"The pigs!" she announced.

I watched Mr. McDog rub his chin and look over at the stack of plastic pigs near the door. There were at least ten of them hogging up the corner near the door.

"Well, maybe" he said, "but the fake horses are bigger. I want the Catfields to do some serious duckin' when we go airborne!"

"But dad," Lilliette protested, "the pigs will fly farther! Just look at them. They're smooth! They're round! They're stream-lined!"

Mr. McDog took another look. "You know, maybe you're right. They do sort of look ripe for the chuckin'. We might even be able to plop one in their pool. Boys!"

"Yeah, Pa?" Lilliette's three brothers called out from practically next to us.

"Forget those horses for now. Y'all come on over here and each grab a big pig."

As the McDog boys put the horse back down and walked away, we let out quiet sighs of relief. In less than a minute, they and their sisters were loaded up with catapult ammo and marching back out the door. Lilliette marched out with them but doubled back when the coast was clear.

"You see, Crew? You see? The whole thing's about to blow! You've got to do something!"

We glanced at one another. It was clear we all had the same thought—Lilliette was nice enough, but her father seemed to be rowing his boat with only one oar in the water.

"Uh . . . right," Keisha said to Lilliette. "Let's go, Crew!"

To be completely honest, I thought about

suggesting we all go back to the train and hide some more, but since Derek and Megan were following Keisha out the door, I went along, too. As we left, a nervous Lilliette called out behind us, "and remember, Crew, whatever you say, don't tell my family I called you here! Otherwise, they'll use *me* for catapult ammo! They have really awful tempers!"

Needless to say, that didn't exactly make me feel better.

CHAPTER FOUR

A Flying Pig?

Now I'm all for a good, straight-forward adventure, but this case was beginning to look a little complicated. Was the feud really a serious fight, or were the Catfields and McDogs more like circus clowns putting on a show for themselves and their neighbors? It was true they were going to fight with catapults instead of guns, but still, those plastic animals weren't exactly light. I tried to imagine what would happen if one of them landed on somebody. At the very least, it would break some bones. Maybe even worse! I decided the whole thing must lie somewhere between really serious and really silly. Dangerous enough for someone to get badly hurt, but still innocent enough for there to *be a chance at a peaceful ending. In short, the situation was balanced like a see-saw, ready to tilt either way. By taking the case, the Crew and I could do our best to make sure everything slid toward the happy side.*

We walked across the McDog's property to the place where their land met the Catfield's. It was in the middle of a big apple orchard that grew up on both sides of the line. As we got closer, we could hear the sounds of drills and hammers getting louder. Soon, we could hear angry shouts as well . . .

"Wow, just listen to all that racket," Keisha said from a few yards ahead of us. The apple trees were planted close together, so it was easiest to walk single file. Keisha was up in front, followed by me, then Derek, then Megan.

"What did you say?" I heard Derek ask.

"I said it's really loud up ahead," Keisha answered without turning around.

"Oh," Derek said. "It's hard to hear with all

that crunching behind me."

"Crunching?" Keisha called out.

"Megan's helping herself to an apple," he explained.

I could hear her, too. The apples hanging from the trees were still green and sour looking, but Megan didn't seem to mind. She had plucked one from overhead and chewed on it as we walked.

"Apple core!" I heard her call out with her mouth semi-full.

"Baltimore," Derek responded at once.

"Who's your friend?" Megan asked.

"Curtis!" Derek said.

I knew what was up. My big sister had played that game with me when I was a kid. So, without even looking around, I ducked down low. Just in time, too. An apple core came whizzing over my head and splattered against the back of Keisha's thigh.

"Whoops. Sorry about that," Megan said as Keisha turned around and put her hands on her hips. "I was aiming for Curtis," she added as if that were a good excuse.

But before Keisha could say anything, a loud, strange sounding 'KA-CHUNK' cracked the air. None of us were quite sure what it was, but we soon found out. I was the first one to see it coming in over the apple trees.

"Look out, Crew!" I shouted. "A flying pig!"

Derek and Keisha dove for cover at once. Megan, however, forgot to put two and two together and stood her ground. I guess she was thinking I wanted to get her back for that missed apple core.

"Oh come on, Curtis," she said. "Do you really think I'd fall for that one?"

I didn't have to respond. Derek reached back up and grabbed Megan's arm, pulling her behind an apple tree just in time. A plastic pig came crashing down less than two feet from where she'd been standing.

"Oh! A *plastic* flying pig!" Megan gasped. "Why didn't you say so?"

"I didn't think I had to," I replied.

But Megan wasn't even listening. Instead,

she suddenly got that determined look in her eyes that happens whenever she gets angry and means to do something about it.

"That does it!" she said. "C'mon, Crew! We have to stop these guys before they hurt someone!"

"Yeah," I nodded. "Like us!"

CHAPTER FIVE

Good (De)fences Make Good Neighbors

With Megan charging full speed into the thick of the battle, there was nothing the rest of us could do but follow behind and lend support. We ran past the last few rows of apple trees and into the clearing where the two farms came together. In place of the low wooden fence that formerly divided the two farms, the McDog kids and the Catfield kids were busy building a pair of giant concrete walls! Already, the cinder blocks stood ten feet high and stretched about twenty feet long on the Catfield side, and at least thirty feet long on the McDog side. Meanwhile, not too far behind, the grown-ups were putting the finishing touches on their catapults. The flying pig that had almost hit us was just the McDog's first test launch. Mr. and Mrs. McDog were now turning their catapult around to face the Catfield's property. And the Catfields, for their part, were busy doing the same.

As we followed Megan to the wooden fence and straight into the center of the whole mess, I couldn't help but notice two older people. They were sitting on each side of the line under big umbrellas. On the McDog side, the elegant looking woman turned out to be none other than Lady Margaret McDog. On the Catfield side, the well-dressed gentleman was Colonel Stonewall Catfield. These were the very two people who had started the feud long ago! Since everyone was either busy working or trading insults, no one seemed to notice us until Megan climbed up on the fence, put her fingers to her mouth, and whistled long and loud . . .

"Okay everybody!" Megan yelled. "That's enough! Stop what you're doing right now!"

I felt my stomach sink into my shoes as everybody turned suddenly quiet and looked toward us with definite hostility. After all, from their point of view, we were trespassers.

"Who are you?" Mrs. Catfield called out suspiciously from her catapult a short distance from us.

"We're the Kinetic City Super Crew," Keisha responded. "We've come to investigate the barn burnings."

"How did you hear about those?" Mr. McDog asked in a voice that practically growled.

"Um, we heard about them on Radio W.A.R.N." Derek answered honestly enough.

"Yeah," Keisha said, jumping in quickly. "It's all over the airwaves."

"Are they talkin' about what a bunch of low down hounds those barn-burnin' McMutts are?!" Mr. Catfield yelled out.

"What?!" Mrs. McDog's face grew beet red.

"Why you Ratfields are the barn-burnin' boogers around here!!"

"Barn-burnin' boogers are we?" the Colonel repeated from beneath his green umbrella, looking straight over at Lady Margaret. "Well, at least we Catfields have enough decency to show up for our own weddings!!"

"I'm glad my horse ate rotten apples that day," Lady Margaret hollered back from beneath her red umbrella. "It kept me from *marrying* one!!"

"I'm glad your horse got sick, too! That old nag saved me from getting stuck with another!"

"Ooh!!" Lady Margaret hissed, visibly shaken. She reached into her glass of lemonade and threw a piece of ice at the Colonel. Luckily, it barely cleared her own shoes.

"Say, whose side are you Super Crew kids on anyway?" Mr. Catfield yelled out.

Derek stood up with Megan on the fence and held up his hands to calm the situation. "Hold on, everybody! We're not on *anybody's* side! We're here to figure out how those fires started in the first place."

"Exactly," Keisha said, backing him up. "We don't think it's arson at all, and we're here to prove it."

"And that means you don't have to use your catapults!" I said.

"Or build those ugly concrete walls!" Megan added.

"Good fences make good neighbors, young lady," Mr. McDog responded, giving Megan a look like she was still too young to understand. He didn't know Megan. She wasn't the type to back down.

"Mr. McDog," she said sharply, "a ten-foot high, reinforced concrete wall with razor wire is not a fence!"

Mr. McDog glanced over at the small section Lilliette's brothers and sisters had already completed.

"You're right," he said, turning back to Megan. "I take it back. Good fortresses make good neighbors!"

Mr. Catfield called out from the other side of the line. "It also makes a nifty fire wall to keep you mutt-faced McDogs from burnin' our whole farm!"

That got them started again. The air was filled with more angry shouts than after a bad call at a baseball game. Megan put her fingers in her mouth and whistled even louder than the first time. It's really impressive how loudly she can do that.

"Excuse me," she said when all had grown quiet again, "but let's make a deal here. If we can't crack this case by sundown, then we'll clear out and you can have your feud."

"Maybe," Mrs. McDog said. "But what's in it for us?"

"Think about it," Keisha said. "If we can prove it's not arson, then there's no reason to fight."

"And everybody can get back to running their farms," Derek added. "There's got to be a ton of work to do around here."

"That's true," Mrs. Catfield called out.

"We've been so busy with the catapult, we haven't had enough time to milk the cows."

"Our milk's better!" Mrs. McDog yelled out.

"Is not!" the entire Catfield clan hollered back.

"Is too!" the McDogs responded.

"Is not!"

"Is too!"

"Is not!"

"Is too!"

Megan whistled for the third and last time.

"Listen everybody," she said when all was quiet again, "we're going to need just a little cooperation, okay?"

"Well, if you kids can't see that the Catfields are barn burners, then maybe you're nuttier than my pecan pies," Mrs. McDog said.

Frankly, the Catfields *and* the McDogs seemed a little nutty to me. But, since we were heavily outnumbered, I decided to keep my opinion to myself.

"We'd like to ask you some questions about

your ex-barns, the Ultra Comfort Suites," Keisha said, doing her best to ignore Mrs. McDog's remark.

"Sure," Mr. Catfield called out. *"Fire away!* Heh heh heh. You see there papa? The McDogs can destroy a Catfield's barn, but they can't destroy a Catfield's sense of humor."

The Colonel nodded proudly. "That's my boy," he said.

Keisha paid no attention to the two men and pulled from her shirt pocket the list we had made.

"Um, does anyone smoke on your farms?" she asked.

Mr. McDog was the first one to speak up. "Not anymore," he said. "The last smoking McDog was old Uncle Micky McDog, and he quit the day he bought the farm, if you know what I mean."

"And no one smokes on our farm either," Mrs. Catfield called out. "Cigarettes give you *dog* breath. McDog breath!"

"Well, that counts out cigarettes," Keisha

said. "What about the weather yesterday? Was there any lightning around here?"

"You bet," Mrs. McDog said. "Big storm blew right through. I even saw a lightning bolt hit the barn."

"Ah-ha!" Megan said, "so lightning *did* strike the barn!"

"Well, yeah," Mr. McDog broke in. "But it didn't start any fires, that's for sure. It hit the barn's lightning rod, and went straight on into the ground, safe and sound."

"Our lightning rod was bigger!" Mrs. Catfield called out proudly.

"Oh, so both barns had them," Megan said, sounding a little disappointed. "So I guess you can strike lightning, Keisha."

"Check," she said as she made the mark.

"What about flammable materials?" I asked hopefully. "Did anybody store any gasoline or paint thinner in those barns?"

All the Catfields and McDogs shook their heads.

"Wasn't anything stored in our barn except

a bunch of hay," Mr. McDog spoke up.

"Same here," Mr. Catfield called out. "Only we had a lot more hay than they did!"

Keisha marked out that one, too. "Well, that leaves bad wiring," she said. "Did those Ultra Comfort Suites have electricity?"

"Of course," Mrs. McDog responded. "How else could we run the CD players, hot tub, and air conditioners?"

"Wow," I said. "Talk about on-the-job comfort. How do you get any work done?"

"It ain't for us," Mr. Catfield called out from behind me. "All that stuff is for the cows! We pampered them with relaxing music, warm baths, and cool stalls set at sixty-eight degrees all summer!"

"Sixty-eight?!" Mr. McDog gloated triumphantly. "Hah! We had our AC set at sixty-seven! And we served mints!"

Derek held up his hands before everyone had a chance to start yelling again.

"Look," he said, "it doesn't matter whose barn was colder."

"Sure it does!" Mr. McDog broke in. "To sell to Mellow Milk, you gotta have some really comfy cows. And ours would've been the comfiest. Course, it's a good thing I hadn't moved them in there yet. They would've, heh heh, lost their cool! Get it? Get it? Lost their cool!"

Mr. McDog bent over sideways as he began laughing at his own joke.

"Heeeheeehee!" he laughed in between gasps for air. "Lost their cool?! Heeeheeheee!"

"That was a good one, sugar plum," Mrs. McDog said, coming over to thump him on the back and help restore his wind.

Lady Margaret called out to us from under her umbrella. "You see there young people? McDog jokes are funnier than Catfield jokes."

"No they're not," the Catfields yelled back.

"Yes they are!" the McDogs replied.

"No they're not!"

"Yes they are!"

Keisha held up her hands again. "Please, everybody," she said, "can we get back to the question about the barns' wiring?"

"Sure we can," Mr. McDog said. "But I don't think there was a problem with it. That system was one of the best money can buy, with triple-reinforced insulated wiring."

"It wasn't a bad wire," Mrs. McDog added. "It was a bad apple on the other side of the fence. Not that I'm naming names—Catfields!"

We huddled up as the family insults started flying back and forth once again.

"Wow," I whispered, "keeping these two families from fighting is like trying to stop a flood with a teaspoon."

We heard Mr. McDog's voice rise above the rest.

"Hey honey bunch! Load me up another plastic pig! I want to send one flying through the Ratfield's roof at sundown!"

"Ugh," Derek whispered through his teeth. "Are these people goofy or what?"

"No kidding," Keisha agreed. "Still, now that we're here we'd better help. Even if they're only flinging plastic animals at each other, someone could really get hurt."

"Well c'mon," Megan said. "We don't have much time. It'll be sundown in a few hours."

"Let's break into teams to cover more ground," Keisha suggested.

"Good idea," I said. "Megan and Derek can check out the McDog's ex-barn. Keisha can take a look at the Catfield's. And I'll go back to the train and coordinate your movements on the Can-Do Communicator!"

From the way they rolled their eyes, I could tell they didn't like my suggestion.

"You come with me, Curtis," Keisha said.

"Okay" I said reluctantly. "But only if I can bring my gadget pack along."

Keisha shook her head and groaned. She didn't understand my habit of carrying a back-pack full of inventions with us on a case.

"Okay, Curtis," Keisha said. "Let's go get your high-tech security blankets."

"Hey!" I said, looking to Derek and Megan for some help. But they were too busy laughing. Little did they know that the very inventions they loved to make fun of were about to help us make a big discovery.

CHAPTER SIX

Friend or Foe

Keisha and I went back to the train to get my backpack full of inventions and then headed for the Catfield place. Meanwhile, Derek and Megan went to investigate the McDog's ex-barn to see what they could learn. While reloading the catapult, Mrs. McDog had told them where to find the remains of the Ultra Comfort Suite. To get there, they'd have to walk along the fence line through the apple orchard and take a right when they got to an old unused building called the Apple Barn . . .

"Hey Megan," Derek said as they tromped across twigs and leaves and a few fallen apples, "are you sure this is the right way? It seems like we've been walking for half an hour."

"Hold on, Derek," she said, squatting down and breaking into an excited whisper. "I think we've found it. Look over there!"

Derek crouched down beside Megan and peered in the direction she was pointing. Through the last few rows of trees, they could see a young man with a ponytail and a tie-dyed tee shirt. He was squatting down beside an old barn. From Mrs. McDog's brief description, they knew it had to be the Apple Barn. It was big and red and had a huge front door shaped like an apple. About a hundred yards off to the right, just like Mrs. McDog had said, they could also make out the pile of ashes that used to be the family's Ultra Comfort Suite.

"What's he doing?" Megan whispered.

"I'm not sure," Derek replied. "It looks like he's trying to drill a stick into that board."

Megan furrowed her eyebrows in that way she does when she's confused.

"Is that some kind of dairy farmer thing or something?" she asked.

Derek shrugged his shoulders. "Don't ask me. I'm a city kid, too. I get milk from the supermarket."

Megan was about to say something else, but was cut off when the young man started to shout excitedly.

"All right! Finally!!"

Megan and Derek watched wide-eyed as he put his stick down and began to fan a small flame with his hands!

"Derek!" Megan whispered as loud as she dared. "So it really is an arsonist after all! Look at him! He's come back to torch a third barn!"

"Fire!" the young man cried out as the flames began to grow. "Yeeeee-Hah!"

"He's going to set the Apple Barn on fire!" Megan continued. "We've got to stop him!"

"Right, Megan. Okay, I'll circle around and . . . hey!" Derek stopped in mid-sentence when he noticed Megan was already up and running. He followed her immediately and caught up just in time.

"Upf!!" the villain grunted as Derek and

Megan pinned him to the ground.

Megan quickly noticed that the flame was coming from a small pile of twigs and not the Apple Barn, but she kicked it out anyway. With Derek still holding the young man down, Megan stood back up and spoke in her toughest TV cop voice.

"All right, hot fingers! You've been busted red handed!"

"Wha . . . ?" he managed to say, communicating as best he could with his face in the grass.

"You have the right to remain silent," Megan continued. "Anything you say can be used against you in a court of law!"

"Are you the Super Crew?" he asked meekly.

"Huh?" Megan said, completely caught off guard.

"How do you know who we are?" Derek demanded.

"Lilliette told me you were coming. I'm Robby Joe Catfield!"

"Well then double shame on you!" Megan said. "Lilliette trusted you. What is she going to say when she learns you're the arsonist?"

"WHAT?!" Robby Joe yelled.

"You heard me, mister!"

"I don't know what you're talking about! I'm not an arsonist!!"

"Yeah, right," Derek said. "You just play one on TV."

"I wasn't burning the barn. I was doing my own investigation!" Robby Joe protested.

"Your own investigation?" Derek asked suspiciously.

"Uh huh! And I think I may have figured out how the barns caught fire!"

Megan and Derek looked at each other uncertainly.

"You do, huh?" Megan said. "Well then, why don't you show us?"

"How can I when I'm pinned to the ground?" Robby Joe answered.

"That's a good point," Megan agreed. "Maybe you should let him up, Derek."

"Yeah!" Robby Joe said. "Maybe you should let me up."

"Okay, but I'm not buying the experiment story," Derek said as he got off Robby Joe's back.

Robby Joe brushed some grass off his colorful shirt as he stood up, too. "I guess it did look pretty suspicious — me starting a fire like that."

"I couldn't agree more," Megan said a little coldly.

"But don't you see?" Robby Joe continued, pointing at the stick and board he used to start the fire. "I just showed how those fires could have started. The Ultra Comfort Suites were made out of wood!"

"So?" Derek asked.

"So," Robby Joe said, "if I can rub wood together to make a fire, then maybe the wind could do the same thing!"

"You mean the wind could have blown so hard the walls of the barns rubbed together?" Megan asked.

"Exactly!" Robby Joe said. "It's called friction. When things rub against each other, it makes heat."

"Yeah, so?" Derek asked skeptically.

"It's been really windy around here the last few days," Robby Joe explained. "And the barns weren't quite finished. I remember seeing some of the hardwood trim just hanging there, swinging back and forth with the wind. Maybe the wood rubbed together so much, it caught on fire."

"I agree with you about friction making heat, Robby Joe," Derek said. "But it sounds really unlikely that wind could make enough friction to start those fires. Just look at how hard you were working to get one going."

"Well, it's not a perfect theory," Robby Joe admitted.

"But what I want to know," Megan said, the suspicion still plain in her voice, "is why you were doing your friction experiment beside the McDog's Apple Barn."

"Two answers," Robby Joe replied in his

own defense. "Number one, this is where Lilliette and I are supposed to meet in a few minutes. And number two, this isn't the McDog's barn."

"It isn't?" Megan said.

"I'm confused," Derek admitted. "Aren't we standing in the middle of the McDog's farm?"

Robby Joe shook his head. "Nope. You're standing right on the property line. In fact, the old Apple Barn straddles both sides about fifty-fifty."

"But how did that ever happen?" Derek asked. "Was it built before the feud started?"

"Nope," Robby Joe said. "Just the opposite. Some guy showed up here after he'd heard about the feud. A few days after Lady Margaret and Colonel Catfield's busted wedding."

"Who was he, a gun for hire or something?" Megan asked.

Robby Joe shook his head. "Not at all. He was a peacemaker. He promised the feud would end if we planted apple seeds between our farms and shared the harvest. The Apple Barn was built to be a symbol of cooperation as well as a place to store the fruit."

"Did it help?" I asked.

Robby Joe shook his head again. "Nah, not for long. But the apples sure are good. And speaking of apples," he continued, his voice sounding suddenly high and squeaking, "I think I see the blossom of my eye! Hey darlin'!"

Derek and I turned around and saw Lilliette coming through the apple trees.

"Hi, Derek. Hi, Megan." she said as she gave Robby Joe a big hug. "You found our secret meeting spot, huh?"

We both nodded.

Robby Joe spoke up again. "But it won't be our spot for long though. Our parents are planning on tearing this old Apple Barn down and putting up those stupid concrete walls right through the middle of the orchard!"

Megan and Derek took another look at the Apple Barn. It still seemed big and sturdy. All it needed was a fresh coat of paint and a little tender loving care.

"Maybe my theory about the wood is a long shot, Crew," Robby Joe said. "But Lilliette and I are sure no one in our families started those fires. There's got to be some other way they could have started."

"Hmm," Derek said slowly, the way he talks when he's thinking of different things at once. "Maybe you're right, Robby Joe."

Megan turned toward Derek.

"Maybe something's going on that we haven't asked ALEC about yet."

Derek nodded in agreement.

"Well, come on, Megan," he said. "Let's go check out what's left of the Ultra Comfort Suite and see if we can find any clues."

"Right," she agreed. "We still have half an hour before we're supposed to meet Keisha and Curtis back at the Control Car."

"Good luck, Super Crew!" Lilliette said, as we waved good-bye and turned to go. "We're counting on you!"

"Right," Robby Joe added. "The sooner this mystery's solved, the sooner Lilliette and I can tell our families we're engaged! Oh, and no hard feelings about the mistaken identity."

"Thanks," Derek replied.

As Robby Joe pulled his hand from his pocket to shake on it, a book of matches fell out and landed on his shoe.

"Heh, heh," he laughed a little nervously as he bent down to pick them up. "I collect match-book covers. I forgot I still had these on me."

"Oh, right." "Of course," Megan and Derek responded.

If Robby Joe could've seen their faces as they turned to walk away, he would have noticed that suspicion was written all over them.

CHAPTER SEVEN

The Dog Days of Summer

While Megan and Derek were confronting Robby Joe at the Apple Barn, Keisha and I had gone back to the Lab Car to get my favorite inventions and start our part of the investigation. We still weren't sure what we were looking for, but, whatever it was, we knew we had to find it quickly. We headed straight for what was left of the Catfield's Ultra Comfort Suite. To save a little time, we took a short cut by climbing over a fence and walking across a huge field of strawberry plants . . .

"We should be getting close now, Keisha," I

said. "I think the Catfield's ex-barn is just on the other side of those trees."

"You call that close, Curtis?!" Keisha replied with a sly smile, the look she always gets when she's about to make one of her puns, "it's still looks *berry, berry* far to me."

I rolled my eyes and tried to pretend I hadn't heard. It didn't work, of course. When Keisha makes a pun, she makes sure anyone within a hundred yards knows about it.

"Get it, Curtis? Get it? A strawberry field?" she giggled. "Berry, berry far?"

I didn't answer. Not because I didn't think Keisha was funny, but because I was too worried about something else, namely, snakes. I have an allergic reaction to them. They cause me to run fast in the opposite direction. I had heard somewhere that they like strawberries, but I wasn't sure if that was true or not.

"Hey, Keisha," I asked, stopping in my tracks. "Do snakes eat strawberries?"

"Upf!" she grunted as she bumped into my backpack.

"Hey, why did you stop like that?" she demanded. "I think I hurt my nose."

"Sorry about that," I whispered. "But I think there's a snake hiding under that strawberry plant over there!"

Keisha immediately forgot about her hurt nose.

"Which one?" she asked.

"The one up there," I whispered back.

"Oh, the one up there, huh?" Keisha's voice sounded a little sarcastic, "Curtis, there are only about a *million* strawberry plants up there . . ."

She broke off her sentence when one of the plants a few rows up ahead started to shake from side to side. I was right. Something was definitely on the other side of it.

Keisha lowered her voice. "Do you think it's a snake?"

"I don't know," I said as I took off my Super Crew baseball cap. "Let me see if I can scare it away."

I grabbed the hat by the bill and flung it

like a frisbee. It was a pretty good throw, plopping down beside the plant that was shaking.

ARF! ARF!

"Hey!" Keisha said laughing. "Either we've discovered the world's first barking snake, or there's a dog behind that bush."

At the sound of Keisha's laughter, a beagle puppy with dirt on its nose hopped over the plants and came running straight for us.

ARF! ARF!

"Run, Curtis!" Keisha tried to scream, but she was laughing too hard. "It's a puppy snake!"

Embarrassed, but relieved, I smiled at my own mistake. "I guess I deserved that."

ARF! ARF!

The puppy seemed to agree.

"Hello, little fella," Keisha said as she picked it up. "You're just a fuzzy cutie-pie, aren't you?"

The puppy promptly licked her on the face.

"Hey, that tickles," Keisha giggled and gently set the floppy-eared hound back down. The puppy took that as the signal for playtime to begin. It turned around and bounded off in the direction of my hat.

"Hey, it's running away," Keisha said.

"No it's not," I responded when I saw what the puppy was up to. "It's going after my cap!"

The dog scooped up my hat in its mouth and dragged it along the ground as it ran down the long rows of strawberry plants.

"Oh no!" I yelled out. "It took me months to fold the bill just right!"

"He probably thinks you threw it because you wanted to play," Keisha commented.

"Well, come on!" I called out as I ran after the four-legged cap-napper. "Help me catch him!"

"No problem!" Keisha said confidently as she sailed past me. Even though she's only a ninth grader, she's a genuine athlete and runs track on the high school varsity team. I think some of that has to do with the fact that she also plays the saxophone and can hold her breath longer than anyone I've ever known.

In any case, by the time I finally caught up on the far side of the field, Keisha and the puppy were already plopped under a tree playing together.

"Hey slow poke!" Keisha called out good-naturedly as I came limping up. "I was about to send the dog out looking for you."

"Hah hah," I said. "You know I can't run as fast as you. Besides, I've got five inventions in my backpack and the Thermo-launcher strapped to my shoulders."

"Excuses, excuses," she said.

"Never mind that. Did you get my hat?"

"Sure did," she said as she handed it to me. "The puppy autographed it with a little slobber."

"Wonderful," I quipped, wiping it off in some leaves before putting it back on.

"His collar says his name is Buford McDog," Keisha added.

"Oh, a McDog dog, huh? Does that puppy know he's on the Catfield side of the fence? Maybe he's a spy."

"Maybe he just thinks the feud is dumb," Keisha said thoughtfully.

ARF! ARF!

"See?" Keisha said. "Buford thinks the feud is dumb."

"Maybe, Keisha," I agreed. "But he's not barking at us. He's barking at whatever's in that big pile of stuff."

Keisha looked over her shoulder to see what I was talking about. Buford was nose deep in a big, brown pile of mulch and digging frantically.

"Yeah," she said with a smile. "Puppies really *dig* mulch. Get it? Get it? Dig mulch?"

"Hilarious, Keisha. Only one thing."

"What's that?"

"What's mulch?"

"Chopped up leaves and wood chips," Keisha responded. "My dad and I spread it around our bushes at home. It helps keep moisture in the soil."

I walked out from under the shade of the trees and back into the warm sunshine where the mulch pile stood.

"What'cha digging for, little buddy?" I asked. I was going to pat him but I never got the chance. All of a sudden, the puppy ran away yelping!

Keisha watched his little fuzzy legs carry him toward home before turning back to me.

"Gee, Curtis, you sure have a way with animals."

"But I didn't even touch him," I responded innocently.

"Maybe there's something in the mulch pile that hurt him," Keisha suggested.

I carefully waved my hand over the hole Buford had dug. It felt really warm.

"Or," Keisha added, "maybe a rat bit him."

I quickly yanked my hand back. A rat bite was the last thing I needed. But something about how hot that pile was started the wheels turning in my head.

"I want to check something out," I said.

"Oh, come on, Curtis," she responded. "You got your hat back. We have to go check out the barn."

"This will only take a second," I promised, unstrapping my Thermo-launcher and putting it on my shoulder.

"Curtis, what are you doing with that overgrown thermometer?"

"Seeing how hot that mulch pile is. It felt really warm, and I didn't even put my hand in."

"Well, *duh*! Of course it's warm," Keisha said. "It's over eighty degrees out here today."

"But it felt a lot hotter than eighty in there," I answered.

CLICK!—I pulled the trigger. KA-CHUNK!—the thermometer came flying out the barrel. THWUMP!—it sank deep into the pile of mulch. Keisha looked a little impatient as I reeled the thermometer back in and checked the digital readout.

"Wow!!" I said when I saw the temperature.

"Don't tell me," Keisha said as she rolled her eyes. "Eighty-something degrees right?"

I shook my head. "Uh uh, Keisha. Higher."

"Ninety?" she guessed.

I showed her the thermometer so she could read it, too. Despite herself, she was impressed. The inside of the mulch pile was two hundred and two degrees!

"Now aren't you glad I brought my Thermo-launcher?" I asked.

Keisha still wasn't convinced.

"Oh yeah, Curtis," she said a little skeptically. "We never could have cracked the case without it!"

"Cracked the case?" I said, blinking in confusion. "We cracked the case? I must have missed something."

"Sure, Curtis," she laughed. "Hot snot, or the case of the blistered beagle."

"Ha ha," I said.

"Now come on," Keisha said seriously. "Let's go look for clues that'll help us with the *real* case. If the Catfields and McDogs start flinging things tonight, we may not get another chance tomorrow."

CHAPTER EIGHT

Getting Warmer . . .

After Derek and Megan's unexpected meeting with Robby Joe, they had more questions than ever. And not just about Robby Joe's theory that friction could have started the fires. There were deeper, darker questions about the young man in the tie-dyed shirt. For example, was Robby Joe telling the truth when he said that he was doing his own investigation? Maybe history was repeating itself. Maybe Robby Joe had cooked up some bizarre plot for revenge. After all, Lilliette's grandmother had left Robby Joe's grandfather standing alone at the altar and looking foolish. Was Robby Joe now trying to do the same to Lilliette?

And what about those matches that fell out of his pocket? Did he really collect them or was that just a quick-thinking excuse on his part? We'd have to keep our minds open for any possibility.

After saying good-bye to the young couple at the Apple Barn, Derek and Megan went and took a look at what was left of the McDog's Ultra Comfort Suite. There wasn't much to see. All that remained was a dark hole in the ground that looked like the world's biggest ashtray. They decided to go back to the KC Express and ask ALEC about friction and fire. That's where they met up with us. Keisha and I had just returned to the Control Car after checking out the Catfield's luxury barn. The only thing left of it was the metal lighting rod, poking up from the ruins like a forgotten flagpole. In fact, the place was so totally destroyed that Keisha and I weren't able to find a single clue. That was a big problem. We needed some clues so we could come up with the right questions. That's how we crack our cases.

Asking the right questions is the only way ALEC the computer can give us the exact info we need . . .

"Welcome to the Control Car," the train door said as Derek and Megan got back on board. "Did you have a nice time?"

"Excuse me?" Megan said. She should have just kept on walking like Derek.

"Did you have a nice time?" the door repeated casually. "Forgive me for asking, but ever since Curtis increased my memory, I've begun to get a little bored with my job here on the train."

"Oh, I'm sorry," Megan said as she shot me a disbelieving look. It was obvious she just wanted to walk away, but that would be rude.

"It's not that I'm complaining, you understand," the door continued before Megan had a chance to move. "I take tremendous satisfaction in helping you and the rest of the Super Crew move through the train as you solve your exciting cases. Still . . . Open. Close. Open.

Close. You must imagine how dull that becomes for a door as smart as me."

"Actually, I haven't really thought about it," Megan admitted.

"My computer chips are barely used."

"No doubt."

"And you'll do something about it?" it asked.

Megan looked at me again.

"Oh yes," she said.

"Perhaps even give me some of ALEC's memory chips," the door suggested eagerly. "That way I could help you with your cases, too."

"I'll definitely bring it up with Curtis."

The door seemed satisfied.

"So, well then, I guess that's it for now. Maybe I should just go ahead and close myself up."

"Wonderful," Megan said.

"Okay. Well, good-bye then."

"Good-bye."

SWHOOOOSH!!!

As the Control Car door shut, the rest of us couldn't help but laugh.

"Who's your new friend, Megan?" Keisha joked.

"Very funny," she said. "But Curtis is the one who packed the doors with that fancy voice activation program."

"Come on, Crew," Derek said. "We can debate doors later. Right now we have some questions for ALEC."

"You do?" Keisha said, raising her eyebrows and sounding hopeful. "What's up?"

"On our way to check out the McDog's exbarn," Megan responded, "we ran across Robby Joe Catfield, and did he ever look suspicious!"

"Why? What was he doing?" I asked.

"We caught him making a fire by twirling a stick in a board," Derek answered. "It looked like he was trying to burn another barn down."

"Yeah," Megan nodded. "Only he says he was doing his own investigation. But I'm not convinced."

"Starting a fire by rubbing wood together?" Keisha said, sounding a little suspicious herself. "What kind of investigation is that?"

"He says it proves his theory that the wind could have started the fires by rubbing the barns' boards together," Megan said.

"It doesn't sound right to me," Derek added. "But I know who we can ask around here to find out."

"The door?" I joked.

"Very funny," Derek said. "Actually, I was thinking of ALEC."

"Right," Keisha said as she sat down in front of ALEC's main keyboard and brought him to life.

"Heeellllloooo Crew!" he chirped as happily as ever. "Did you know that fire needs oxygen to survive, just like you do? Without oxygen, most kinds of fires simply go out. That's why water, dirt, or a wet blanket can put out a fire—it suffocates the flame. Since our conversation this morning, I've been downloading all kinds of interesting fire facts!"

"Uh oh," I said. "He's getting ready to spew out a list!"

It was too late. ALEC was on a roll. When he gets excited like that, it's hard to cut him off.

"The control of fire was critical for human evolution. It allowed people to do things like cook foods that couldn't be eaten raw, or keep wild and savage animals at bay, or harden the points of wooden spears, or make clay pots as hard as stone, or light the cave at night, or . . ."

"ALEC!!!" we all yelled.

There was a single, soft beep.

"I let myself get carried away, didn't I?" he said.

"It's okay," Keisha said. "We know you get excited. But we need to get some specific information from you."

"That's right," Derek said. "We saw for ourselves that fire can start just by rubbing wood together fast enough."

"Yeah," Megan spoke up. "Could the wind ever do the same thing? I mean, could it ever blow hard enough so that the barn rubs against itself and catches fire?"

"Checking!" ALEC called out and began to beep. Three seconds later he let out a DING! "Negative, Crew! To start a fire by rubbing wood together, the friction must be highly concentrated on a single spot."

"Oh," Megan said. "So that's why Robby Joe was twirling the stick in the board. It concentrated the friction."

"Precisely," ALEC confirmed. "If the boards in the barns' walls were rubbing together, the friction would be too spread out to cause a fire."

"So Robby Joe's barking up the wrong tree," Derek said. "Either way, though, he's still our suspect number one."

"And speaking of number one," Keisha said sadly, "I'm afraid that's the square we're still on."

"Maybe," I said. "But there's still the question about the mulch pile."

Derek and Megan looked at me quizically.

"What mulch pile?" they said at the same

time, sounding like stereo speakers.

Keisha answered before I could say anything. "Oh, Curtis used that thermo-thing to take the temperature of some old mulch."

"Yeah," I said, defending my invention. "And I found out it was almost hot enough to boil water in there. How can it get so hot all by itself, ALEC?"

"Checking!" our computer called out and beeped frantically. After a couple of seconds he let out a DING! and an answer that would surprise us all.

"Mulch, which is dead plant matter such as chopped up leaves and wood chips, doesn't get hot by itself at all!"

"But ALEC," I protested, "I took the temperature with my Thermo-launcher. It was like an oven in there!"

"I believe you, Curtis. But you asked me how mulch gets hot by ITSELF, and the answer is—it doesn't. Instead, it has a practically countless number of little helpers called bacteria!"

"Oh, bacteria," Keisha said as we all nodded. "We've all heard of them."

"You see, Crew," ALEC continued, "as the bacteria rot the dead plant matter, they generate lots of heat. If the pile is moist, the bacteria will multiply and rot the mulch faster. This generates even more heat. Sometimes, the heat can actually reach the mulch's ignition point and cause the whole pile to burst into flames!"

"Wow!" we all said.

"Fascinating, huh?" ALEC said before continuing. "The whole thing's called *spontaneous combustion*. It can be a definite safety hazard if it happens in a home or business."

"What about a barn?" I asked.

"Of course," ALEC said. "Any building with a rotting mulch pile inside of it would be at risk."

"Well all this mulch trivia is truly fascinating," Megan said a little sarcastically, "but what's the point? The McDogs and Catfields didn't have mulch in their barns. Just a bunch of hay."

"Actually Megan," ALEC responded, "hay is a lot like mulch. If it gets moist, it creates heat as it starts to rot and break down. If conditions are right, the result can be spontaneous combustion!"

"And a barbecued barn!" Keisha added excitedly.

"Wow! That's got to be it!" I yelled. "Both the Catfields and McDogs had a ton of hay in their barns! You see, Keisha? My Thermo-launcher came in handy after all!"

"Well, I don't want to throw cold water on your parade, Curtis," Derek said. "But how would the hay get wet *inside* the barn?"

"Maybe there was a leaky water pipe or something." I suggested. "You even said yourself there may have been a problem with the way they were made."

"Well, it's too late to find out now," Megan said. "All that's left of those barns is a big pile of ashes."

"Hold on," Keisha said. "I know where we can go see an Ultra Comfort Suite for ourselves! C'mon Crew! I think it's time to pay a visit to the Paradise Barns company!"

CHAPTER NINE

Lots of Hot Air

Finding Paradise Barns wasn't difficult. It was easily the biggest business in Vegtaville, with an outdoor showroom set up right in the middle of town. All the different barn models were on display in a humongous parking lot. At first, we weren't quite sure where to go, but then Derek noticed a sign that read 'Main Sales Office' on a large barn near the back. It was a bright red, triple-decker surrounded by lime green, artificial grass and plastic barnyard animals bolted into the asphalt. There was a pink horse having its hooves manicured by a mechanical chicken, some orange goats sitting at a picnic table playing checkers, and a huge, yellow cow sitting in the middle of a giant hot tub. We walked up *to the front door, and Megan rang the metal triangle that dangled there on a rope . . .*

CLANG-A-LANG-A-LANG!

"Hey, that triangle's in the key of 'C,'" Keisha said.

"Good ear, Keisha," I said with a grin. "Maybe you could switch it for your saxophone."

"Hah hah, Curtis," she replied.

"Ahem," Derek cleared his throat in that way he sometimes does to remind us we're in the middle of a case. "I don't think anyone heard us, Crew. Maybe you should give the triangle another ring, Megan."

"Right," she said and tapped on the triangle's sides once again.

CLANG-A-LANG-A-LANG-A-LANG!

"HELLOOO!" a deep, loud voice boomed out from behind us. "And welcome to Vegtaville's leader in luxury, farm animal accommodations!"

Since the voice came from behind us, we

all turned around and expected to see some salesman standing there. Instead, there was nothing but the life-sized plastic farm animals we had passed while walking up.

"Remember," the loud, deep voice continued, "once you've bought the farm, you're going to want a Paradise Barn!"

"W-who said that?" I called out a little nervously.

"I'm not sure," Keisha said, cupping a hand to her musician's ear, "but I think the voice is coming from that plastic cow in the hot tub."

Derek walked up closer to it as the loud, deep voice continued.

"Buy a barn while the blue light's on, and save lots of MOOOOOOO-LA!"

"Yeah," he called out. "Keisha's right. It's coming out of this one."

"There must be a tape recorder in there," I observed.

"A tape recorder nothing!" a fast-talking voice called out as the sales office door swung wide open. "Son, I'll have you know that plastic cow is stuffed with the latest in digital surround sound technology!"

We turned back around and saw a smallish man wearing a purple, checkered sport coat and a neon orange bow tie.

"How ya doing, customers?" he spoke quickly, stepping forward and shaking our hands. "Chuck Roast's the name."

"Hi, Mr. Roast," Keisha tried to say. "We'd like to ask you abo . . ."

"About the great deals I have for you?!" he broke in quickly. "Ma'am, I like the way you think! Skip the small talk, let's get down to business!"

Mr. Roast pulled a pointer out of his jacket pocket and, stretching it out full length, thwacked the side of the barn he had just walked out of. "Now just feast your eyes on this beauty here!"

He pointed at me.

"You there, young man, now what would you call this marvel of artistic architecture?"

"Um . . . a barn?" I guessed.

Mr. Roast looked a little hurt.

"A barn?! Son, this isn't just a barn! Why, it's a certified slice of bovine heaven! Comes fully equipped with hot tubs and wide-screen, Cowtronic cable TVs in every stall."

"What would a cow possibly want to watch on TV?" Derek asked skeptically.

"The Green Grass Channel, of course! Just think, Bessy can kick back in the comfort of her own stall and watch field grasses growing in real time twenty-four hours a day!"

"Gosh," Derek said, rolling his eyes, "sort of makes me wish I were a cow, too."

Mr. Roast nodded enthusiastically. "Doesn't it?! Doesn't it?! And, for a slight additional charge, we can install automatic, flavored salt lick dispensers, tasty cow treats now available in sweet clover, green onion, and lemon grass!"

Even though I was trying my best to be polite, I couldn't help but wrinkle my nose at the idea of flavored salt licks. And I wasn't even sure what a salt lick was. Mr. Roast saw me and nodded sympathetically.

"I know what you mean. I don't particularly like the salt licks myself. They make me thirsty. I promise you, though, cows can't keep their slimy tongues off of 'em!"

"The barns sound really wonderful, Mr. Roast," Keisha said, finally getting a word in edgewise. "But we're not farmers."

"What?! Not farmers?" he called out in surprise. "You mean I've been pitching with no one at the plate?"

We all nodded.

"Yes, I'm afraid so," I said.

Mr. Roast furrowed his brow for a brief moment before shrugging his shoulders.

"Oh well, doesn't hurt to practice I guess. But if you were farmers, you would've bought one of our Paradise Barns, right?"

We all nodded again.

"Oh yeah, without a doubt," Keisha assured him.

"Maybe even two," Megan spoke up. She had genuine appreciation for a good salesman.

This seemed to make Mr. Roast feel better. He smiled just like before and pleasantly asked us a question.

"So then, if you don't want a barn, why are you here?"

"We're the Kinetic City Super Crew," Derek responded. "We've come to ask you some questions about the barns you sold the Catfields and McDogs."

"Oh," Mr. Roast said. "You mean the Ultra Comfort Suites."

"Exactly" I said.

"The Biltmore Mansion of barns we call 'em. You see, your average barn is just one big old room. And it's a real hotbox in the summer, I can tell you. That makes for some stressed out cows."

"And Mellow Milk only makes dairy products from comfy cattle," Megan added.

"You got it," Mr. Roast confirmed. "That's why we put up a wall in the middle of the Ultra Comfort Suite with an air conditioner right in the center of it."

"An air conditioner for cows?!" Derek asked in amazement.

"You bet," Mr. Roast answered as though the idea didn't seem the least bit odd. "Mellow Milk wants their cows to be cold chillin'! That's why the Ultra Comfort Suite is designed for the cows to stay in the air conditioned half while all the hay and farm tools stay in the other."

"Oh," Keisha said, trying to understand, "but why divide the barns like that in the first place?"

"Because," Mr. Roast explained, "we only need to keep the cows cool. Anything more would just be a waste of energy. Of course, it does get pretty hot in the hay storage room with that AC exhaust blowing over it, but what the heck. Who needs cool hay?"

"Yeah, *that* sure would be a useless luxury all right," Derek said, doing the best he could to keep a straight face.

"Exactly!" Mr. Roast said before clapping his hands together. "But kids, why are we talking when we could be gawking? Let's go take a look at the Ultra Comfort Suite. It's just two barns down on the left." He pulled a chain out of his pocket with about a thousand keys on it. "It's the hottest barn ever made!"

We'd soon find out just how right Mr. Roast was.

CHAPTER TEN

A Fire Sale

Even though he seemed a little weird, Chuck Roast was nice enough to take the time to show us the Ultra Comfort Suite. The model was an exact copy of the kind of barn that both the Catfields and McDogs had bought. We walked over and met back up with Mr. Roast at the Ultra Comfort Suite's huge front door . . .

"You kids sure are in for a special treat," he announced proudly. So, are you ready to put yourself in a bovine state of mind?"

"Excuse me?" I asked.

"Are you ready to put yourself in a bovine state of mind?" he repeated.

"How do we do that?" Megan asked.

"*Why* do we do that?" Derek asked.

"Don't 'cha see?!" Mr. Roast chirped like a cheerleader at a pep rally. "The whole point of a Paradise Barn is to make cows cozy! If we try to understand things from a cow's point of view, we'll see just how ultra sweet this barn really is!"

"Well . . . since you put it that way," Derek said uncertainly. "I guess it makes some sense."

"Sure it makes sense!" Mr. Roast exclaimed. "Okay, since I've done this plenty of times before, allow me to prepare the MOOOOOOOd!"

"To prepare the what?" I asked.

Mr. Roast repeated his cow noise for us, only this time even louder.

"The MOOOOOOOOOOOOOOOOOOOOd!"

"Oh." I said. "The mood."

But Mr. Roast didn't even seem to hear me. He was too busy doing knee bends and taking deep breaths. When he finished, he was all set for a cheer that would help put us in the bovine spirit.

"Ready!?" he shouted, waving his arms in the air like they held pompons. "Okay!"

"We've spent all day in the heat and mud making cow patties and chewing our cud!

We've stared into space with our big cow eyes standing in the sun and swatting at flies!

We've been chased by doggies who think it's fun to see how fast an old cow can run!

But the sun's going down and our work day's through!

If you want to see the barn, give a great, big MOO!"

"MOOOOOOO!" Keisha, Megan, and I shouted out. Mr. Roast sure was goofy, but, I had to admit, he was a pretty good cheerleader.

"There now! That's the bovine spirit!" Mr. Roast said as he looked encouragingly at Derek. "And what about this young bull here? HEARRRD enough?"

Looking at us for a moment like we had totally lost our marbles, Derek finally shrugged his shoulders and gave his serious nature a brief rest.

"Moo," he said with a smile.

"YAY!!" we all cheered as Mr. Roast dramatically threw open the barn doors and led us in.

We had heard that the Ultra Comfort Suite was the ultimate in fine cow living, but it still didn't prepare us for what we saw when we went inside. Giant crystal chandeliers hung down from the ceiling and lit the barn in a rich, golden light. The floor was covered with wall-to-wall carpet, and giant, cow-sized furniture was arranged tastefully around the barn. I was the first to speak after the initial shock wore off.

"Cow-a-bunga!" I said. "This place is a palace!"

"Sure is," Mr. Roast agreed, barely able to contain his excitement. "Okay, imagine that you've just spent a long, hot day in the fields. You're all sweaty and your lips are green from munched up grass and slobber. Now, what would be the first thing on your mind?"

Derek shrugged his shoulders. "Well, since you put it that way, I guess a bath would be a good idea."

Mr. Roast shook his head. "That's close. But remember, baths are for cows living in ordinary barns. This is the Ultra Comfort Suite! Here we have something extra special."

Our host moved to the middle of the room and grabbed a blue velvet curtain that covered up a large object.

"Tah dah!" he shouted as he yanked it away. "Behold! The very latest in comfy cow technology!"

We all gasped, too impressed at first for words. Finally, Keisha was able to get a few out.

"Is that what I think it is?" she asked. "A hot tub for cows?"

"Oh no," Mr. Roast said dramatically, pleased to have made such an impression on us. "This isn't just some run-of-the-mill hot tub. No-sir-ee! Why this baby here's an authentic, turbo-charged Mooocuzi! Cows go nuts over them. But don't take my word for it! Let's ask this happy camper right here."

Mr. Roast pushed a button, and, as the

water started to churn around in the giant tub, the life-sized plastic cow sitting in it suddenly came to life, moving its head up and down.

"Mooooooo!" it said from a speaker partly sticking out of its mouth. "That feels gooood!"

"It's all very impressive, Mr. Roast," Derek admitted. "But what we'd really like to see is the hay storage room."

"Oh, we'll get to that," our host chirped, as happy as a little kid in a candy store. "But first let me show you our patented Moooosagers and those flavored salt lick dispensers!"

"Mr. Roast," Keisha spoke up in her firm but pleasant voice, "that's very nice of you, but what we'd REALLY like to see is the hay room."

"Oh. Okay," he said, sounding a little disappointed. "But it's so hot in there and cool in here. I mean, just look at that AC blasting away, would you?"

Mr. Roast pointed toward the wall that completely divided the swanky part of the Ultra Comfort Suite from the hay room on the other side. Sure enough, stuck right in the middle of it was an air conditioner humming away. Keisha walked over and took a look.

"It's set on high," she remarked.

"You bet," Mr. Roast responded. "There aren't any real cows in this barn, but there sure are a lot of customers."

Derek walked over beside Keisha and pointed to the small door in the wall.

"Is this the entrance to the hay room?" he asked.

"Sure is," our host said. "But there isn't much to see back there."

"The handle's warm," Derek said as he turned it.

"Well, like I said," Mr. Roast replied, "it's a real hot box back in that hay room. I reckon if farmers wanted cool hay, we could build a Deluxe Ultra Comfort Suite and stick an AC back there, too." He rubbed his chin at the thought. "Hmm, you know, that might not be such a bad idea."

Derek didn't pay him any attention. Instead, he called out to us, the excitement in his voice unmistakable. "Hey Crew, come check this out! I think I've found something important!"

We rushed into the hay room to see what he was talking about. As we did, the heat hit us like a slap in the face.

"Wuuf!" Megan said, "it's totally burning up in here!"

"Look," Derek said, pointing at the big pile of hay on the floor. "It's steaming!"

Chuck Roast popped his head in the door behind us but didn't come in. "Ugh," he said, "see what I mean? This is the kind of heat that gives barns a bad name. Come on back in where it's cool, and I'll demonstrate our patented mooosager."

"Wait. Hold on a second everyone," Keisha said suddenly. "Look at the back of the air conditioner!"

We all turned around to see what Keisha was pointing at.

"There's water dripping out of it," I said. "And it's getting on the hay!"

Mr. Roast shrugged his shoulders. "Yup, that's the thing with air conditioners. You're always going to get a little condensation dripping out the back. I guess that accounts for all the steam in here." He scratched his head. "Hmm, that just gave me an idea, with all this steam, maybe we could turn this room into a sauna for the cows . . ."

I turned toward our host and tried to clue him in. "Mr. Roast, you don't understand. If that wet hay gets hot enough, this whole barn could be char-broiled!"

"Uh oh!" I heard Megan coughing behind me, "I think it already is! That isn't steam coming off that hay—it's smoke!"

"Smoke?!" Derek shouted. "That mean's the pile could reach ignition temperature any second!"

"And burst into flames!" Keisha called out.

"Do you have a fire extinguisher, Mr. Roast?" Derek asked, his voice tense.

"A fire extinguisher?" Mr. Roast shook his head. "Paradise Barns didn't become the leader in deluxe farm animal accommodations by wasting money on useless luxuries . . ."

WHOOOOSH!!!!

"Flames!" Keisha shouted as the hay pile suddenly glowed bright orange.

"Let's get out of here!" Megan called out though it was a little unnecessary on her part. We were already on our hands and knees crawling out the door. As we all made it into the cool air of the main room, we stood back up and ran to safety outside. For the first time ever, I outran Keisha.

CHAPTER ELEVEN

Tempers Flare

It was a good thing we got out of the Ultra
Comfort Suite when we did. Before I had even
finished calling the fire department on my cell
phone, huge orange flames were already
shooting from the roof. By the time the fire
trucks arrived a few minutes later, the whole
barn was one giant ball of orange, capped by
thick, black smoke that rose high into the
air. With so many sirens blasting away and
with the smoke sending a signal for miles
around, practically the whole town of
Vegtaville soon showed up to watch. As for
ourselves, we stepped back to join the crowd
and looked on as sweaty firefighters rushed by
with hoses, gas masks, and axes . . .

"Whew!" Derek whistled through his teeth. "What an inferno."

"I know what you mean," Keisha nodded in agreement. "I can feel the heat on my face from here."

"If you think we're warm," I said, "check out those plastic farm animals. They're turning into puddles."

The life-sized models Paradise Barns used for decoration had become nothing more than multi-colored globs of goo. We stood and watched some purple chickens and lime-green goats blend together until a deep, angry sounding voice suddenly bellowed out from close behind.

"So, yuh couldn't keep your barn-burnin' bottom lyin' low for a while! Could you? You spark-settin' slug head!"

"Me?!" a voice just as angry shouted back. "You're the one with a barn-burnin' bottom, buster!"

"Don't call my husband buster, buster!" an irate-sounding woman screamed out.

"Very well!" a second woman replied, just as nastily. "Then how 'bout we call your husband the barn-burnin' butthead instead?!"

"Uh oh," I said nervously, "is that who I think it is?"

Derek turned around and took a look. "Yep," he nodded, "the Catfields are squaring off with the McDogs, all right."

"Uh oh!" Keisha said urgently. "C'mon, Crew! We have to clear things up quickly!"

Keisha began to run toward the angry couples with the rest of us trailing close behind. Even though we came right up to them, they were so angry with each other that they didn't even notice us.

"Very well," Mr. McDog said, rolling up his sleeves, "it looks like we're going to have to settle this dispute like adults. C'mon Ratfield! Tag team wrestlin'! Right here and now!"

"You're on, McMutt!" Mr. Catfield growled as he rolled up his own sleeves.

"I'm gonna give you a double whammy belly slammy!!" Mrs. McDog hissed as she stepped toward Mrs. Catfield. "Just to see how high you'll bounce!"

"Oooh!" a furious Mrs. Catfield hissed right back, "you just had to go there, didn't yuh? You just had to go there!"

Just when the situation threatened to get completely out of hand, Keisha did the bravest thing I've ever seen anybody do. She stepped right in the middle of the feuding families and held up her hands.

"Wait!" she yelled as loud as she could. "Don't fight! We think we've figured out how BOTH of your barns caught fire!"

The Catfields and McDogs stopped in the middle of their tracks and looked at Keisha as though she had just landed from outer space.

"Huh? What? Wuh? You do?!" they said.

Keisha knew she had to use their momentary confusion to explain the situation as quickly as possible. Otherwise they'd be at each other's throats again.

"We've found the answer: HAY!" she yelled.

A good try, but it didn't help. The

Catfields and McDogs were still confused. Mr. McDog's eyebrows knotted as though Keisha had just asked him to do long division in his head.

"Um, hey what?" he asked and blinked a couple of times.

Megan stepped in quickly to give Keisha a hand.

"No," she said, shaking her head, "HAY as in the stuff COWS eat. The fire started in the HAY!"

That time they understood. Or, at least I thought they did.

"Oh, the HAY," Mr. Catfield said as he rubbed his chin and nodded knowingly.

"That does make perfect sense, doesn't it? McMutt here set fire to my hay."

His comment was less than helpful. No sooner were the last words out than the whole dispute was flaring up again.

"Why, you lie like the varmint you are, Ratfield!" Mr. McDog bellowed, his face beet red.

It was Derek's turn to step in. "Hold on everybody! The air conditioners you had in your barns were dripping water on the hay."

"And moist hay can catch fire if it gets hot enough!" Keisha added quickly. "It's called spontaneous combustion."

"Yeah," I said. "We just saw it happen! That's how the show barn caught fire!"

That one did the trick. We could almost see the anger deflating from their faces like hot air escaping from untied balloons.

"Uh . . ." Mr. Catfield said, searching for words. "So it, um, wasn't . . . a little neighborly sabotage after all?"

"Well, I'll be," Mrs. McDog said. "We didn't even think about the AC making the hay wet, did we, dear?"

Mr. McDog shook his head. "You're right, honey bunch. We didn't. I guess you all can color me embarrassed on this one. I've . . . I've wrongly accused you, Catfield."

Mr. Catfield shuffled his feet in the gravel. "No, no," he said. "I'm the one who was too hotheaded here. I wrongly accused you, too."

Mrs. Catfield stepped forward and took

Mrs. McDog by the hand. "I'm sorry for all those nasty things I said about your pies at the bake sale, Betty."

"It's okay, Sally May," Mrs. Catfield responded, "I'm sorry for not paying back those quarters I borrowed at the laundrymat."

Seeing that their wives were now made up, Mr. McDog took a deep breath and looked Mr. Catfield squarely in the eye.

"Well, what are we waiting for, neighbor? Come here and give me a big hug!"

Mr. McDog and Mr. Catfield stepped forward and gave each other a big hug complete with three firm thumps on the back with their fists.

"Well, I think these Super Crew kids have taught us all a valuable lesson," Mr. Catfield said as he stepped back. "Listen, McDog, instead of feuding . . . let's be friends."

"Aw, that's so sweeeeet," Keisha said, touched by the spirit of the moment.

Mr. McDog felt it, too. A little tear even appeared in the corner of his eye. "I'm . . . I'm touched, Catfield," he sniffed. "I really am. From now on, let there be nothing but goodwill in Vegta-VILLE!"

Mr. Catfield nodded enthusiastically. "Wonderful! I couldn't agree with you more, my new best friend. Only, one little thing, our town isn't pronounced Vegta-VILLE. It's Vegta-VUL."

Mr. McDog smiled politely, but he shook his head. "No, my dear friend. You're mistaken on that one. It's Vegta-VILLE."

Mr. Catfield started tapping his foot like he was getting impatient. "I hate to differ with you, buddy of mine, but we Catfields have been living here for a hundred years and it's pronounced . . . Vegta-VUL!"

Mr. McDog's eyes narrowed to two little slits. "Well, chum, we McDogs have been living here for a hundred and FIFTY years, and it's Vegta-VILLE!"

"Vegta-VUL!" Mr. and Mrs. Catfield shouted.

"Vegta-VILLE!" Mr. and Mrs. McDog shouted back.

"Vegta-VUL!"

"Vegta-VILLE!"

"Vegta-VUL!"

"Vegta-VILLE!"

"Oh brother," Derek said, rolling his eyes.

"I guess our work here is done," I said, wondering how far of a walk it was back to the train.

Megan looked at the freshly feuding couples. They ignored us completely as they shouted at each other as angrily as ever. "I guess you're right," she said. "Maybe when the firemen are finished putting out that fire we can ask them to give these goobers a good hosing down."

CHAPTER TWELVE

A Hot Case's Cool Close

We were glad we had cracked the case and proved it wasn't arson. But we still felt bad that we hadn't been able to do anything more for Robby Joe and Lilliette. As it turned out, we didn't have to worry. A couple of weeks after we got back to Kinetic City, we were in the Kitchen Car having lunch when ALEC came on to announce the hot line was ringing . . .

"Helllooo, Crew!" he chirped.

"Mmmph," we said as we tried to say 'hello' back. Like a waiter in a restaurant, ALEC had caught us at the exact moment our mouths were totally stuffed with mushroom pizza. ALEC didn't seem to mind. In fact, I had even programmed him to understand muffled speech.

"My sensors inform me the KC hot line has now rung three times, er . . . make that four times. Shall I answer it and put it on speaker phone in here?"

"Pleath ALECth," Keisha said, taking a quick sip of soda.

We heard the phone click from the speaker on the wall as Keisha spoke up at once.

"Kinetic City Super Crew, when you want the facts, we hit the tracks, Keisha speaking."

"Hi, Keisha!" a familiar sounding voice called out, "this is Robby Joe Catfield!"

It was immediately followed by another.

"And Lilliette McDog! We've got some great news."

"What is it?" I asked.

"The feud is over!" Robby Joe called out happily.

We all put down our slices of pizza and

began to applaud. Megan clapped so hard some tomato sauce flew off her fingers and hit me on the nose. Under normal circumstances, I would've fired back with a mushroom or two. But, because this was a happy occasion, I simply wiped it off and let it slide.

"That's really great news!" Derek chimed in. "But how did it happen? Your parents still seemed so mad when we left."

"Well, it all has to do with that Mellow Milk competition I told you about," Lilliette said. "With all the Ultra Comfort Suites burned down, there was no barn left to win the contract."

"Until Lilliette and I secretly fixed up the Apple Barn. You remember, the one beside the apple orchard," Robby Joe said.

"Sure," Derek said.

"You see," Lilliette added, "after you all figured out the problem with the air conditioner, the rest was pretty easy. Robby Joe and I turned that barn into a new and improved version of an Ultra Comfort Suite."

"And," Robby Joe added, "Mr. Roast gave us all the fancy equipment we needed to make up for selling our families bad barns in the first place."

"So?" Keisha asked hopefully, "are you guys saying . . ."

"Not only are we getting married," Lilliette said happily, "but Robby Joe and I have won the contract with Mellow Milk! Soon all the milk for the best ice cream in Kinetic City will come from our comfy cows!"

"That's great!" Derek said congratulating them. "But what do your parents think about this?"

"Well, once we showed them the Mellow Milk contract and the fancy new barn," Robby Joe answered, "they agreed to divide the farms in a good way."

"Exactly," Lilliette said. "Only not with stupid concrete walls, but with a brand new farm of our very own! Robby Joe and Lilliette's Dairy Farm!!"

"YEAAAH!!" we all cheered.

"And guess what?" Lilliette added happily. "We've even convinced Colonel Catfield and Lady McDog to start courting again! Who knows? We might even have a double wedding!

"But even if we don't, you all are definitely invited to ours!" Lilliette said.

"Great," Megan responded. "But I don't know what to bring for a gift."

"Oh," Lilliette said, "after what the Super Crew has done, you don't have to bring anything."

"Aw, that's so sweet," Keisha said.

"Of course, if you do," Lilliette added quickly, "I guess we could use a fire extinguisher."

It was a good thing Robby Joe and Lilliette were on the phone so that they couldn't see Derek shake his head and roll his eyes. The rest of us smiled because we all knew exactly what he meant—'oh brother!'

We all said good-bye to Lilliette and Robby Joe until the wedding. The case of the barbecued barns was now officially closed. The only hot item before us now was our pizza, just the way things should be.

THE END

Home Crew Hands On

Fire Drill

Dear Home Crew,

A few days after we got the call from Robby Joe and Lilliette that all was well, Keisha and I were in the Lab Car checking out my latest invention, the Cookie Zapper. Things got a little out of hand. Here's exactly how it happened.

"So what's this thing supposed to do, Curtis?" Keisha asked, poking at the device on the table with some uncertainty.

"It'll bake cookies as fast as lightning," I said.

"It looks like an old bug zapper."

"It is an old bug zapper."

Her nose wrinkled immediately. "I'm not eating cookies baked on a bug zapper!"

"Relax," I said. "It was never even used. I found it in the back of the Supply Car, still in its box."

Keisha didn't looked convinced. "Well, even if it *is* clean, dropping raw cookie dough on it doesn't sound like a safe thing to do. You're just asking to get burned."

"But that's the beauty of it, Keisha," I explained. "Your hands never get close to the electrified bars. See? The safety screen's on."

Keisha examined the wire mesh and saw that it was still in place. There was no way to touch the glowing purple bars, even if you wanted to.

"All right," she said, "but how do you get the cookie dough in?"

I turned the Cookie Zapper around so she could see the other side. That's where I had installed a little swivel window, like the kind at drive throughs of fast-food places.

"You see, Keisha," I said. "It's simple.

Simply place the cookie dough on the pan. Put the pan on the swivel window. Turn it around so the dough comes into contact with the electrified bars and *presto*! Instant chocolate chip cookies!"

Keisha didn't say anything.

"Would you like to congratulate me now, or wait until you've tried one of the cookies?" I said, fishing for a compliment.

Keisha still looked skeptical. "I don't think these things should be used for cooking, Curtis."

"Aw, come on, Keisha," I said. "This is an *experiment*. Besides, this isn't cooking. It's baking."

"Whatever."

"Would you like the honor of making the first batch?"

"Well," she said, "it's against my better judgement, but, if anything goes wrong, it's your mess to clean up, agreed?"

"Agreed," I said.

Keisha dipped a spoon into a mixing bowl

full of cookie batter and plopped a decent sized chunk onto the pan.

"Okay, here goes nothing," she said, swiveling the window around.

As we quickly learned, Keisha was wrong about it being nothing. The result was definitely something, but not the something I expected.

"It's burning!" Keisha yelled as smoke began to gush through the safety mesh.

I quickly turned the window back around so that the batter would no longer be in contact with the bars. It didn't do a whole lot of good. The batter stuck.

"Flames!" Keisha shouted. "Pour water on it!"

"No!" I yelled. "Not on an electrical fire! Use baking soda!"

"Well, at least unplug it first!"

That was a good idea. I grabbed for the cord and yanked it out of the socket. The bars lost their electric glow but the dough continued to burn, filling up the Lab Car with smoke.

Keisha ran over to the shelf where I kept a box of baking soda. I kept it open just in case one of my inventions didn't work out as planned. She rushed back and flung the whole box over the table. A huge, white, powdery cloud choked off the flames at once. We stood silent for a moment looking at the mess.

"I guess that one didn't work so well," I said.

"You can say that again," Kiesha agreed.

"At least it's over."

I was wrong. The smoke alarm went off just as Megan came running into the room, blowing on a police whistle.

"Evacuate!" she yelled after taking it out of her mouth. "ALEC's sensors just picked up a fire somewhere on the train!"

"It's okay, Megan," I said. "The fire's out."

Megan noticed the mess on the table. She looked at it curiously for a moment.

"A bug zapper?" she finally said.

"You don't wanna know," Keisha said quietly.

"But anyway," I said, feeling a little embarrassed, "we don't need to evacuate the train."

"Oh, yes we do!" Megan said. "This accident just convinced me we need a plan to leave the train quickly if an emergency gets really out of hand."

"You mean a fire drill?" Keisha asked.

"Uh huh," Megan responded. "I've got my watch on so I can time us. Let's just pretend the Lab Car's still on fire."

That wouldn't be too hard. A cloud of smoke clung to the ceiling and a burning smell filled the air.

"Ready?" Megan continued, looking at her watch. "Go!"

Keisha was into it at once. "Quick, Curtis, run to the door!"

"Wait a sec!" I said. "The windows are closer!"

Keisha ran over and tried one. "Ugh! This window is stuck! Let's go back to the door!"

"Wait!" I said. "Let me get the rest of the cookie dough!"

"Hello?" Megan called out, tapping her foot on the floor. "This is an evacuation . . . not a picnic!"

"Exactly, Curtis," Keisha added with a giggle, "you'd be *batter* off to leave it behind! Get it? Get it? Batter off?"

Megan blew her whistle again. "Okay, okay. Forget it. You two are pitiful."

"Well, gee, Megan," Keisha said, "how are we supposed to make a speedy evacuation if we don't even know what the evacuation plan IS?"

"Exactly," Megan said. "That's why this is the perfect time to read you this."

She pulled a slip of paper from her pocket.

"What is it?" I asked.

"An evacuation plan," she answered. "What we should do in case of fire. I was going to suggest we try this later, but you guys seem to have come up with a good time for it on your own."

"So what's it say?" Keisha asked.

Megan read. "First, in case of fire, you should leave the train as quickly as possible.

Don't stop for anything!"

"Not even my saxophone?" Keisha looked a little upset at the idea.

"Not even your *wallet*!!" Megan responded before continuing her list. "Second, know the shortest route to the outdoors, and have a backup route in case the first one is blocked by flames or smoke."

Keisha looked around. "So we could go through the front door of the car or the back door of the car. Or the windows."

"But we'll need to make sure those windows open," I added.

"And third," Megan continued, "in case of a fire, crawl on your hands and knees to your chosen exit."

"To stay below the smoke level," Keisha said.

"Anything else?" I asked.

Megan looked back at her list. "For the last part of your evacuation plan, choose a place outside where everyone agrees to meet. If you live in a house or apartment building, you might choose to meet across the street. Once you've left your home, go straight there so everyone would know you're okay."

"Well," Keisha said, "since this plan is for the train, maybe we should meet about 100 yards away from the left side of the caboose?"

"Okay," Megan said. "It's a plan. Everyone agreed?"

Keisha and I shook our heads.

So that's how the Super Crew came up with our evacuation plan. A little goofy on my part, huh? I never thought about the dough sticking to the electrified bars like that. Anyway, does your family have an evacuation plan? If not, why don't you design one yourself? It's easy. Just figure out the shortest way to leave your house or apartment from each room. Make sure you also have backup routes. You should also make sure all the windows open easily and have ladders or ropes for rooms that aren't on the first floor.

Once you've designed the plan, practice it with your friends and family and make sure everyone knows it. You should even time your practice evacuations to see how fast you are. Then call or e-mail us with your family's best time. You can reach us at our Web site at www.kineticcity.com. Or, you can call us on the phone at 1-800-877-CREW. That's 1-800-877-2739. If you leave us a message, you might be able to hear yourself give your family's best time on a future Kinetic City Super Crew radio show!

Good luck, Home Crew!

Your friend,

Curtis

Puzzle Pages

Words on Fire

The Super Crew investigate all of their hunches and suspicions before they finally crack the case of the burning barns. Unscramble the words below to see if you remember some of them.

1. ria dceonoitrin
2. lngihtgni
3. irtotgn lmuhc
4. idarasep sarbn
5. ectelcri wginri
6. someksr
7. apitn tnhirne
8. fticiron
9. ewt yha
10. aoiegsln

_____ are the leading cause
(answer is the word in grey boxes)

of accidental fires.

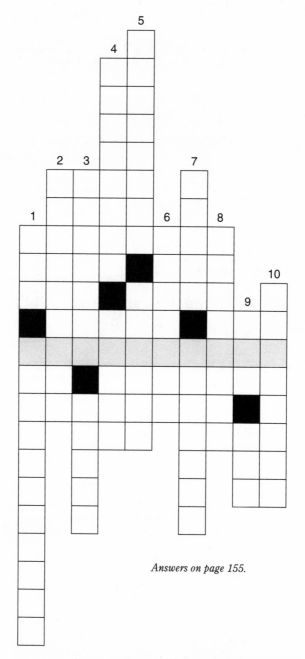

Answers on page 155.

A Little Alliteration

Barn-Burnin' Boogers! That sounds almost as hot as Flamin' Fire! Why do these phrases sound so awesome? alliteration. That's when words right near each other share consonant sounds, like the B's in Barn-Burnin' Boogers.

Fill in the spaces below to spice up the speech!

Lovely (L)◯◯◯◯◯◯◯ was in love with the romantic (R)◯◯◯◯ Joe.

The McDogs and the Catfields are fighting over burned down (B)◯◯◯◯ .

The families both want business from (M)◯◯◯◯◯ (M)◯◯◯ .

Comfy (C)◯◯◯ make the best milk.

Flammable (L)◯◯◯◯◯ or lightning could start a fire.

A playful (P)◯◯◯◯ meets Curtis and Keisha in the strawberry field.

Curtis' Thermo (L)◯◯◯◯◯◯ launches a thermometer through the air.

Answers on page 156

Whacked Wordsearch

Can you find all the words?

berry berry
Chuck Roast
Cyber Car
dairy farm
flashover
ignition point
strawberry field
safety drill
spontaneous combustion
Super Crew

```
f s a f l a s h o e n t k l j i r o n p i o
r c p i o x u y b v d s e e y g u b m y n h
g d o o b u p y t m e o i r p n w z s r v y
s l h m n b e d y t n r g b i i y a u i a e
t w p s b t r c r e w w i s j t t s d t m f
r k i w e u a y t g h c v b n i i t m e m y
a v f h r l s n d e a v s z q o t l p s g r
w r c a r i g t e o n s p o n n f l t e t i
b e k a y v j a i o t k t j v p o i n t o a
e b g b i r d a u o u r s a n j p r w u l d
r y p d y n r a t m n s a f e t y d i n s e
r c n g i t b e j a s s o n g n n t w q o p
y f i e l d u p b w y o r k c u h c n d q i
```

Answers on page 156.

Cool Idea

If you mix vinegar and baking soda, you can make foam and gas like the stuff in fire extinguishers. Why do fire extinguishers spray out foam anyway? Why not just water? The gases in the extinguisher are what put the fire out better! The gas in the extinguisher cuts off the oxygen supply to the fire and fire can't exist without oxygen.

Super Crew instant ideas
just add brain power and stir

Hot Idea

Next time you're outside, see if you can find a pile of leaves that have been sitting around for a while. Like ALEC said, mulch really can get super hot! So if the leaves are mixed in with some soil and other stuff you may find that the inside of the pile is warm. When the leaves start to break down they can get warm even hot! Try it!

Puzzle Answers

Words on Fire

Grid numbers: 1, 2, 3, 4, 5, 6, 7, 8, 9, 10

```
                    5 E
                  4 P  L
                    A  E
                    R  C
                    A  T
         2  3       R      7
         L  R  D    R      P
         I  O  I    I      A
1
A  G  T  S  C  S    I  F
I  H  T  E  ■  M  N  R
R  T  I  ■  W  O  T  I     10
■  N  N  B  I  K  ■  C  W  G
                                 A
C  I  G  A  R  E  T  T  E  S
O  N  ■  R  I  R  H  I  T  O
N  G  M  N  N  S  I  O  ■  L
D     U  S  G     N  N  H  I
I     L           N     A  N
T     C           E     Y  E
I     H           R
O
N
E
R
```

A Little Alliteration

LILLIETTE

ROBBY

BARNS

MELLOW   MILK

COWS

LIQUID

PUPPY

LAUNCHER

Whacked Wordsearch

```
f s a f l a s h o e n t k l j i r o n p i o
r c p i o x u y b v d s e e y g u b m y n h
g d o o b u p y t m e o i r p n w z s r v y
s l h m n b e d y t n r g b i i y a u i a e
t w p s b t r c r e w w i s j t t s d t m f
r k i w e u a y t g h c v b n i i t m e m y
a v f h r l s n d e a v s z q o t l p s g r
w r c a r i g t e o n s p o n n f l t e t i
b e k a y v j a i o t k t j v p o i n t o a
e b g b i r d a u o u r s a n j p r w u l d
r y p d y n r a t m n s a f e t y d i n s e
r c n g i t b e j a s s o n g n n t w q o p
y f i e l d u p b w y o r k c u h c n d q i
```

156

Future Case Files

From Metal Heads:
The Case of the Rival Robots

Marci turned the main controls on and Emma twisted the joystick on the remote. The lights blinked on around Muggsy's middle and we all cheered.

"Muggsy's back!" I yelled.

And then . . . nothing.

"C'mon, Emma, get him going," said Marci. "Give him the juice."

Emma twisted the joystick frantically. "I *am* telling him to move. He's still not working."

Muggsy stood, frozen in place. The blinking lights were his only signs of life.

PJ took the basketball and rolled it gently toward Muggsy. It bounced lazily off him, and rolled away to a stop.

Marci sighed, looking down at the floor. Emma twisted the joystick around and around, as if refusing to believe it wouldn't work. The Thompson twins sighed in perfect unison. And Katie blew a big, fat, purple bubble.

I looked at the other members of the Super Crew, and then at the big clock on the scoreboard. It was less than an hour to Muggsy's spot in the contest. Now that we'd removed what we thought was the problem, we had no idea what could be wrong with him.

From One Norse Town: The Case of the Suspicious Scrolls

I trotted over to help Max. When I picked up a thick textbook called *Medieval Norse History*, I saw something that caught me completely off guard. The book had fallen open, face-down, and when I lifted it up, there was a pile of money underneath it. And we're not talking spare change—we're talking bunches of crisp one-hundred dollar bills!

I turned the book over and saw that someone had carved a big hole in all of the pages, leaving a space to stash the cash. I had no idea what the money was for, but it looked like Max's stomach had led us to our first clue.

"Hey, Crew," I said, trying not to speak too loudly. "Get over here *now*! Look at what's in this book!" I showed them the carved-out pages and the wads of hundreds.

"There must be ten or twenty thousand dollars here!" said PJ, flipping through the bills with amazement.

Up until now, everything had looked pretty normal on the museum's end. But how could we explain *this*?

⟹◈⟸

GET REAL!!

This and every adventure of the Kinetic City Super Crew is based on real science.

The mysterious barn burnings were due to spontaneous combustion. (Robby Joe was let off the hook—he really did collect matchbook covers.) The spontaneous combustion phenomenon is real, and, under certain conditions, can represent a major safety hazard to buildings.

Spontaneous combustion can occur in piles of hay or mulch from the heat produced by the action of countless microorganisms, just as it happened in the story. The phenomenon can also take place in the presence of volatile substances, or what ALEC called flammable liquids in Chapter 2. (If the Crew had thought to ask ALEC about other things that can catch fire by themselves, they might have cracked the case then and there!) These volatile substances, like paint thinner, gasoline, and some furniture polishes, can actually produce invisible vapors that are only one little spark away from an explosion. For this reason, it's very important that all such items be stored in metal containers with tightly closed lids.

The Cyber Car fire in Chapter 3 was inspired by an actual test conducted by Professor Howard Emmons at Harvard University. He left a burning cigarette on a bed in a room and recorded the first flames showing at two minutes. At four minutes, a thick smoke had filled the room. By approximately 7 minutes the whole room burst into flames in an explosion called *flashover*. Flashover happens when things in the room are so hot that they reach an ignition point. The super-heated objects and gases in the room burst into flames. The Cyber Car helps demonstrate that most domestic fires start small and the Crew learn that most often the culprit is a malfunction in an electrical device or a burning cigarette.

As for fire safety, the Crew was smart to create an evacuation plan. No matter how unlikely, unwanted fires are still a possibility, even on the KC Express train. Just witness Keisha and Curtis in the Kitchen Car—good thing they had that baking soda on hand! However, a good evacuation plan is not enough. It's also important to have smoke detectors and fire extinguishers that actually work.

Try the Home Crew hands on yourself and give us a call. We'd love to hear from you!

NOW HEAR THIS!!

Every week tune in to the Kinetic City Super Crew radio show!

If you think reading about the Crew is cool, wait till you hear them blasting out of your radio. Every week the Super Crew find themselves tangled up in danger and mystery ... from icy tundras of Alaska to the busy streets of Kinetic City.

Call 1-800- 877- CREW (2739)

to find out where you can tune in to hear the next awesome episode of Kinetic City Super Crew.

KCSC is featured on Aahs World Radio and finer public radio stations around the country.

AMERICAN ASSOCIATION FOR THE ADVANCEMENT OF SCIENCE

National Science Foundation

Kinetic City Super Crew is produced by the American Association for the Advancement of Science and sponsored, in part, by the National Science Foundation. Opinions expressed are those of the authors, and not necessarily those of the foundation. The *Kinetic City Super Crew*, the train logo, and the associated logo type are trademarks of AAAS.